Patty.

enjoy my brother Dan's book.

ENTITY

A Second Coming

A novel by Steve Shapiro

Entity, *A Second Coming*

ISBN: 978-0-615-40111-9

Written by Steven R. Shapiro
Edited by Victoria Miller
Book design by Courtney Bomkamp; BRIO
Cover photo by David L. Brown

www.EntityASecondComing.com
www.SteveRShapiro.com

Printed in the United States of America

Dedicated to my brother, Daniel Norman Shapiro

ACKNOWLEDGEMENTS

Special thanks to all of my friends who battled through earlier drafts and gave their input and feedback. They are: Tim Bianchi, John Feehan, Ken Irvine, Claudette Lane, Michael Kaveney, Karen Lesto, Tiffany Lindsey, Ron Mulliken, Ray Pogwist, Eunice Riccio and Johnny Rodriguez; also Joann Colo'n for her computer-word savvy and to editor Shveta Thakrar. And to Dean Koontz, a special thanks for taking the time to answer my letter with advice and words of encouragement.

ONE

"Come on, Dan, you've got fifteen minutes to go to the diner with me."

"I'll be ready in an hour, Steve."

"Come on," I repeated. "I'm leaving with or without you in twenty minutes."

Dan is my older brother and I look after him now. He's sixty-one, and I'm fifty-six. He's one of those guys from the sixties who somehow got all messed up in his early twenties and had a series of nervous breakdowns. Before that he was a brilliant student with a very high IQ at the Bronx High School of Science and was just a great older brother to have while growing up in the shadows of Yankee Stadium.

I can remember as if it was yesterday. Standing in the terminal at Newark International Airport thirty-two years ago, looking out of that large-picture-framed-window facing the arriving planes with my parents, eagerly awaiting my brother's return from a Salt Lake City hospital. We watched as every passenger departed the plane onto that old-style step ramp used for outside exiting, until there were no passengers left. We wondered if he was somehow not on the plane, until a stewardess appeared at the exit hatch with an older, stoic-looking figure of a man, held by her arm.

Standing before us in that dank Newark drizzle was a stranger, bearing only a strange resemblance to my twenty-seven year old brother, a caveman, as my parent's cried out in anguish. His eyes had raccoon-like blackened circles, his face was puffed out, bruised and unshaven for at least one week's time. His body was hunched over much like an older man in his sixties. This was all due to the horrific beating that he had received in Utah, while hitchhiking his way back home to New Jersey. For all intents and purposes, this mere shadow of a man was someone else who had taken over possession of my brother, never to be seen again in this lifetime. One life gone and another dream shattered.

The police in Utah said that he was left for dead along the side of a road with broken bones and a concussion. No charges were filed against the two men who said that my brother had wandered onto their property and had helped himself to a drink of their water from an outside spigot without asking their permission. Justice was duly dealt out upon my brother. From that point of time onward, doctors could never be certain, exactly, what caused the ever-changing, ever-lasting damages to Dan, physically, emotionally, mentally and spiritually. Perhaps it was this terrible beating that he received, which rendered him unconscious for a few days? Or, perhaps, it was the many drugs that he ingested and smoked, along with the "tripping" that he took with his head, while living in California for two and a half years, during the sixties-hippie era? Then again, it may have just been his biological genes changing. As my brother had later told me, he felt something going on in his brain in his later teen years Who knew? Not even the doctors could pinpoint it. But I personally felt that it was due to that beating, which probably dislodged his brain to a degree, from some of those vicious kicks to the head that he received from the welcoming committee of "dear old Utah."

My mind snapped back to the present, as my brother was now ready to make his journey to the diner with me, our diner, the Riverside Diner. All that he wanted to do was to sit in this diner for about five hours or so, have something to eat, smoke about twenty cigarettes, and drink approximately eight cups of coffee. It is great therapy for him. He is diagnosed as bipolar, with a dash of depression and mania thrown in. Still, he's a great guy and I love him.

He had lived in Asbury Park, New Jersey on his own for thirty-one years after the incident and had allowed me my space. Somehow, he managed to survive. It wasn't easy for either one of us, but he was resilient. I figured that enough was enough for the guy, as it was not an easy life for Dan. Plus, I always worried for him. How would you feel if you were once on top of the world and suddenly everything was turned upside down? That is why I built him an addition to my house and moved him in after I retired from work.

We stayed at the diner for about an hour and a half, until I couldn't take anymore. Dan had his usual 'something soft,' a bowl of lentil soup, along with five or six cups of decaffeinated coffee, until they ran out of the pot that they had exclusively made for him. I had my mundane and usual cheeseburger deluxe with a coke.

After we left the diner, lightning started to flash. It was eerie. The sky flickered on and off like a light switch, yet there were no sounds of thunder. There were no lightning bolts, either, only flashes that continued for an hour. I thought that I might be going crazy, or hallucinating. It was very humid, too, as if the skies were begging to break out into a downpour. But the rains never came. When it ended, I went inside to hear if there was anything about it on the ten-o'clock news. There was nothing. What the heck was going on?

I went into the den area of our house, which was the designated room that we shared. It was quite like the Israel-Palestine border for us. On my side lied sanity, which I could always come home to. On his side lay some other kind of sanity, which I was not accustomed to, nor was anyone else. His apartment beyond our den was like a nomad desert with items lying scattered around, a dish here, a cup there, an ashtray full of butts filled with water to prevent any possibility of spontaneous combustion. Here, too, lay mysteries still unknown to science.

When you entered into Dan's sanctuary, you stepped into Marlboro country. It reeked of cigarette smoke and had a noxious cloud lingering throughout it that seemed to give the impression of clouds in the sky faintly moving. Dan was sitting at his kitchen table I had picked up from a pizza parlor. It gave him the feeling of being in the diner all the time. He was engaged in one of his smokes. He sat there in his underwear with a watered- down cup of coffee. He was a sight to behold. His face had become folded with lines of pain and despair over his plight. His hair was curly, unkempt, now salt and peppered. But his beard was truly a landmark-- mangy and bushy, with an occasional bit of food thrown in there. He bore a stark resemblance to Aqua-Lung, and I had to love him.

I thought that I heard him talking to himself, which he was inclined to do. I asked him, "Whom are you speaking to?"

"Oh, just to the radio," he said, as he tried to avoid my stare by focusing on his cigarette in the ashtray. I hadn't noticed that the radio was on, but it was, at a very low volume.

"Dan, that's mostly static that you're listening to."

"No, it isn't," he said. "There's some freaky guy that's talking about the dream state that we live in."

He took in a deep inhale on an unfiltered Camel. The smoker's delight drifted up into the creases on his face.

"You're kidding me, aren't you?" I said. He gave me no answer. So I sat for a while to listen to this radio guy. After a few minutes of choking on smoke and hearing nothing but static, I left to go back to my area of sanity. I put on Jay Leno in my bedroom. *What else is new?* I thought, as I fell asleep after the monologue.

TWO

The next day, Dan was taken to his psychiatrist by the medical transportation provided by county human services and Medicaid, for his quarterly appointment.

"Dan Shapiro is here to see you, Doctor Abukabar."

"So, what do you think, Doc?" my brother asked.

"Think about what, Dan?"

"Think about these crazy voices that have been coming on the TV lately?" asked Dan.

"Why don't you tell me about those voices, Dan?"

Dan proceeded to tell the Doctor about all that had transpired since his last visit.

It was shortly after Dan left the Doctor's office and was placed in another cab ride home by Medicaid, that I received a call from Doctor Abukabar.

"So, Steve, your brother is hearing voices," he said.

"Well, that's not unusual, Doc."

"Is he acting any different?" asked the doctor.

"No," I said. "In fact he seems to be more normal than usual, more in touch with himself."

"Okay, Steve, keep an eye on him and give me a call if he's having any troubles."

"Sure, Doc," I said.

Doctor Abukabar picked up his phone and rang his administrative assistant.

"Jenny, let me get through to the State Board of Psychiatry at the Capitol."

He tapped on his notepad until he heard a voice on the other end.

"Jill Prentice, hi, this is Doctor Abid Abukabar down at the southern branch. Listen, I have an incredible number of patients that are hearing voices, lately.

Have you heard anything about this?"

"Yes, Doctor Abukabar, we've been hearing many accounts of this happening, lately."

"What's that you say?"

"Yes, I said. We have been getting a lot of calls about these voices."

"You have to be kidding me. Why hasn't anybody informed me, Jill?"

"Well, we have been so inundated that we haven't had the chance to get anything out as of yet, to our members. And, besides, this is all new to us, too. We are assimilating the information, currently. As it stands, it seems that most of our patients are hearing these voices on their televisions as well as their radios. And most of these patients are of the emotionally-challenged type."

"On the television as well as the radio?" questioned the Doctor. "Yes, Doctor, that's what we're finding. In short time, we expect to get a memorandum out to all of our Board members."

"You're going to get a release out on this," he repeated.

"Yes, as soon as possible. This is more widespread than we expected."

"So, it's been large scale all across the state, I don't believe it," said Abid.

"No, Abid. This is widespread across the nation, not just the state."

"What? You're finding out that this is happening nationwide? What are you going to do, Jill?"

"Well, Abid, that is for our National Chapter to decide. Apparently, they're going to release an article in the *National Journal of Psychiatry*, and do a press release, shortly."

"Oh, I see, in the *National Journal*, and get a press release out," repeated the Doctor.

"No, that's a good idea. I mean, what the heck is going on here, Jill? I've never seen anything like this either."

"I know, I know. But, there is one important thing that we are asking all of our members to do, Abid, and that is to keep this from leaking out to the public. We really don't want to cause a panic, especially, since we're not even sure what we're dealing with here. Okay, Abid?"

"Oh, okay, Jill. I'll keep a lid on this!"

THREE

"It is infinite out there. One is all and all is one, Dan."

"You know that I really enjoy finally talking to someone who will listen to me and is as intelligent as I am," replied Dan.

"Thank you," said the entity.

"You know, your dream state scenario is pretty interesting. I've been thinking about it lately and it could be plausible," said Dan.

"In that case, you think more about it. I am here to broaden your perspective on life and not to tell you what to think."

"But, how can I do that? People are thinking that I'm acting more crazy than usual," Dan replied.

"Dan, what we intend to do is talk to people like you first, since you are the most receptive kind. We know that the others, the so-called normal ones, would not accept us right now. This is a good way to introduce ourselves to your world. We also wanted the psychiatrists to break the story to the newspapers. Believe me, Dan, at first it will look like a big joke. In time, though, we will talk to more people and less will laugh. You know how reluctant your world is about aliens and UFOs. You see, Dan, we don't have flying saucers."

The entity continued, "Instead, we travel free of machines. We are very different from what your planet can imagine. We are even different from how your movies depict us. For we are many, but one, where plural is the same as singular. I,or we, try to open the minds of our hosts. I am more of a spirit form of life, closer to your dream state. Who is to say what is out there in the vastness beyond? Your world believes only what it can see. Dan, there is much more than you can ever imagine in a lifetime. You cannot see me, because I am from other dimensions. It seems as if I exist only to inform others that other life is out there. We have been doing this for as long as we can remember, which is forever."

Dan hesitated and then spoke. "Well, listen, I'm going to have a smoke right now, so how about we talk about this later?"

"Okay, Dan, speak to you later."

FOUR

A week passed, and all of the hoopla about strange voices seemed to have faded away. The weather continued to be hotter than usual, but not abnormally so. I had decided that "out of sight" meant "out of mind". Still, I had a bad feeling that something was wrong. I could not let go of the strange weather phenomena. Under the circumstances, I felt the need to get away with my dog into the mountains for some camping and relaxation.

We loaded up the sixteen- foot travel trailer and headed north. I always loved to travel. Since retiring, I bought myself a small trailer and was living out my urges for peace and traveling.

"Where to now, Oogie?" I asked my Labrador retriever. "How about this place near the town of Deposit in the western part of the Catskills?"

This destination had become a favorite stop of mine. A nice, quiet park to camp in was nearby. For most New Yorkers, it was a bit too far away to get to easily, while for many New Jersey-ites, it remained unknown.

Oogie and I headed north as he majestically sat in the passenger seat. He was very certain that that seat was his and his alone; no one else was getting it.

After four hours of driving we passed through a hamlet called Tudorsville. Two minutes later we entered the park.

"What do you say, Oogie? Should we take a short hike, boy, before it gets too dark?" Oogie knew the word hike, as well as the word walk. They both meant the same to him. His ears perked up as his body wagged from side to side. We were up in the hills, one mile into our sojourn. Oogie walked ahead of me, jingling his bells around his collar.

We were about to turn back since it was getting dark when the bells faded from hearing. This could only mean one thing. He was checking something out, or something terrible happened to him. Being a retriever, Oogie was the type of dog who would always scout ahead of me and then come back, as if to tell me that the coast was clear. It seemed to be a natural trait of his. This time, though, he was not back and there were no jingles. I could feel my anxiety kicking in as I quickened my pace to find him.

As I came over the crest of the footpath, I saw him. He was sitting off on the right hand side of the trail, in the same way he sat in the passenger seat of the van. I approached him cautiously, as I expected that he was staring at some type of animal. Twenty feet away from him, I stopped. I had never seen him sitting in such a trance. He appeared as if he'd become a statue, paying no attention to me. I wondered if he heard something, saw something, or felt something that was unnerving him.

I concentrated to hear or see anything and noticed that the world around me was devoid of all sound. At this point, though, I could feel the hairs on the back of my neck standing up. Most discernibly, I was experiencing fear.

"Come on, Oogie, let's get out of here."

He finally broke from his trance and headed back down the trail with me to our campsite. I set up the trailer and made us some dinner. Neither one of us ate like we meant it. After dinner, we sat in the trailer in silence, except for the hum of our generator. We seemed to be the only ones in the park and I was feeling a bit uneasy, affected by our earlier walk. We must have dozed off around eleven.

At seven in the morning, Oogie was licking my face,

waking me up. It was daybreak and he was ready to go. We both felt better after a night of sleep. Stepping out of the trailer into a vivid sunlit morning, we headed for the same exact trail we took last night. I didn't have to speak; Oogie had the same idea. We began our hike back into the mountain. This morning, the forest was alive with sounds, smells and a gentle breeze. Still, the eeriness of last night's walk was still on my mind. I sensed that something was not right about it. I wondered if anyone else had noticed anything on that particular trail.

At eight-thirty, we found the 1930s-era Maxi Diner on Route 68 in the town of Greenly. It wasn't much of a town. But, I was glad to happen upon it because I was hungry and needed a cup of coffee badly. I picked up a copy of *USA Today* and sat down in a worn torn leather booth. Hardly any cars were passing by, and the town's only business on Route 68 seemed to be the diner and a lumberyard hardware store.

I was the only soul in the diner, or at least seemed to be when, finally, a petite lady in her thirties came out of the kitchen and walked over towards me. She was tough-looking yet pretty. She had brown chestnut hair, half in a ponytail and half hanging loosely.

"My name's Mickey, what can I get you, honey?"

"Well, I can use a cup of coffee, Mickey".

She placed down a menu and smiled, "I'll be right back."

I stared outside of the diner window to the highway. The morning sun had faded into a gray haze with drizzle. After a while, a car flew by and the waitress returned to my booth.

"I'll have one of your country breakfast sandwiches," I said to her as she set down my coffee with a smile. She nodded silently and I picked up the newspaper. When I got to page three, I was startled to see an article from The National Alliance of Health that said psychiatrists across the nation had been noticing an increase in anxiety stress among their patients. At the end of the article, it was noted that most of these patients were of the emotionally challenged sort. Doctors could not say why they were feeling more anxiety, except that it might be due to the changes in weather patterns lately.

Any changes in normality can bring anxiety to challenged people due to their delicate state of mind and well-being. *What a crock of baloney*, I thought. Then I thought back to the conversation I had with my brother's psychiatrist and it dawned on me. Maybe it wasn't just my brother if many challenged people were experiencing strange delusions. *Jeez, I guess my brother is not the only one hearing voices.*

Just then, I noticed that Mickey had been standing next to me holding my sandwich in her hand.

"Boy," she said, "you must have really been absorbed in that article. Is that the one about the shrinks thinking that people are talking to extraterrestrials?"

"Well, yeah and no," I responded. "I mean, they didn't say anything about extraterrestrials."

She nodded, but I caught a glimpse of her pretty green eyes as she stared at me intently and said, "But of course that's what they meant."

"How do you know that?" I asked.

"You see, my husband Billy Joe is not all there, if you know what I mean? And he's been talking to them lately. He's scaring the hell out of me and our five kids."

I began to realize that maybe there was more to it than what it seemed to be. Suddenly, I wasn't as hungry as I thought I was.

FIVE

"So Dan, what makes you think that it's all right to eat animals?"

"Because, it says so in the Bible," was his reply. "God said that He gave all of this earth to man, so that he may flourish and sustain himself."

"But who wrote that, Dan?"

"The prophets wrote that down from the words of God," Dan recited.

"But, Dan, why wouldn't God want to protect all of the living things that He created? Don't you think that these living things have feelings, that some actually have a conscience and can actually figure out more than nothing?"

"Yeah, maybe they do, but that's the way that God made it. Listen, if God didn't want us to eat animals, then why is it all right to eat plants?"

The entity hesitated for an instant. "That's a very good question. I'll try to tell you why. I think it is because you must draw the line of civility somewhere. As I have told you before, I have been traveling forever throughout the heavens above and within. In this thing called time, which is eternity for me, I have not been able to determine if there really is a God. With all of my wisdom gained through infinity, I cannot prove it. I believe that it will never be proven as long as there is life. Perhaps it was purposely set up that way!"

"So, are you telling me that you don't believe in God?" asked Dan. "Are you telling me that God didn't make everything else to sustain us?"

"I do believe in a God, but that is not what I'm getting at. Dan, I believe that God would want you to believe in Him through your heart and your kindness.

Killing is only justifiable to a certain degree. If your greed is excessive, then you act no different than a cancer, or a bacterium. Humans do not appear to be in touch with their surroundings. You could sustain yourself on other forms of matter and energy, such as plants. Humans are therefore abusing their resources, along with their powers."

"So, why is it all right for other animals to kill to survive?" asked Dan.

"That is easy. They have no other choice. Your intelligence allows you to make that choice."

"And you, what do you eat?" asked Dan.

"I consume energy that is around me. You may even consider that this energy is a form of primitive life as well and that I am a hypocrite, too. I am different than you, though. I do not agree with your aggressive concept of killing. My point is this, Dan. There are other forms of life out there that believe in your form of hypocrisy, too. You, though, are their next meal ticket, if they arrive."

SIX

"Doctor Lewis, Secretary of Defense, this is Ramsey Jaffee, National Board of Psychiatry. Ladies and gentlemen, we have been called to this meeting by the President. As you know from your briefing, the Government is quite aware of the phenomena that have been occurring, such as the strange increase in psychiatric counseling for people talking to their televisions."

"Oh, may I interrupt you please, Secretary of State Neary? These people are talking to their radios as well," indicated Doctor Lewis.

"Yes, I forgot to include that, Doctor Lewis. I do want you to know exactly what we are doing and what we expect of you. The President has authorized the Department of Defense to contact this thing, if it in fact exists. So far, though, we cannot. I mean that we have gone as far as listening to televisions and radios but can not get contact."

Doctor Jaffee then interjected, "Well, Secretary Neary, as we have been saying all along, this thing seems to contact only the psychotic, the challenged or the mentally disabled. We do not believe that this is some kind of joke or hoax. There have been too many incidents reported, and it is worldwide, according to my Board of Psychiatry."

"And that is exactly why the President is asking you to provide our Defense Department with some of your patients, so that we can put this thing to rest," responded Secretary of State Neary. "The F.B.I. and the C.I.A. have been checking to see if your reports are authentic and it seems that they are. Also, they have been checking with other countries to see if this is some kind of plot to stir up mass hysteria, but it seems not. Actually, we are much more concerned about what other countries may think and therefore fear the possibility of terrorist reprisals."

"But, Secretary Neary, ma'am, it is against our patients' standard of rights to be involved in such things."

"In that case, Doctor Jaffee, ask them if they care to help their country first and whether they would like to receive a paycheck for their services."

SEVEN

Oogie and I were off into the woods again. I just could not get this traveling thing out of my system. It was starting out as a beautiful day. Up the hills, down the gullies, through the clearings, over streams, dimly lit passageways through sun- drenched meadows. This was the beauty that only a god could make. Oogie and I scanned the view. As I looked down at him, I wondered if he, too, was in awe? How could he be? I bent down to pat him and asked, "What are you doing, boy?"

Not again, I was thinking. He can't be. He just sat there as if he was hypnotized, listening to something. *That's it, he hears something again and I can't hear a damn thing!* But then I heard it too. Although hard to describe, it was an emptiness, a feeling more than the overbearing silence, that made me nauseous and dizzy. It was the lack of sound that struck me.

We were pulling the trailer out of the park and heading home. "That did it, Oogie. I think that we had enough." Not only was the park empty of campers and hikers on a day in the middle of the summer, but it was getting a little bit too scary for my liking. I couldn't get that darn sound out of my head. It filled my mind, but it was a sound of emptiness.

Upon leaving the state park, I leaned outside of my door window to ask the young female park ranger why there were no sounds on the mountain. She wouldn't look up at first, as if she hadn't heard me. After what seemed like an eternity, she slowly turned toward me.

"Oh, that eerie, empty sound? Yes, we've been noticing that for days now and we haven't got a clue. It kind of drives you crazy, doesn't it?"

I said nothing, just turned my eyes back to the road and drove off. While driving home, I was conjuring up images of what that empty sound reminded me of. It was like getting hit in the ear and hearing nothing but the vibration from the ringing. It became nauseating after a while. It was difficult to listen to it for too long, this deafening silence. There was nothing to be heard; no animals, no wind, nothing. It was as if every living thing was too creeped out to make any noise. I knew that I'd rather be home.

My journey home, though, took an unexpected detour. Instead of the normal five-hour drive, it became ten hours. I had pulled over to have dinner and after eating, decided to take a short nap that inadvertently turned into five hours of vivid dreams. I remembered hearing my name being called over and over. Reality had faded into drowsiness as I closed my eyes and drifted off to sleep. I dreamt about my brother when we were much younger.

I couldn't keep pace with him, as his steps were longer and quicker than mine. I had always found myself a good twenty feet behind him, jogging to catch up every now and then. I was only ten years old and he was sixteen. We were headed down to 161st street to get me some new clothes. Dan was always the clothing maven. He could match colors, something that I could never do, not realizing why until I was diagnosed with colorblindness many years later.

Highbridge and Anderson Avenue is where we lived in the Bronx, New York City. Down the long hill, across the Rock Park, past Yankee Stadium, and into the shadows of the elevated number 4- subway line, we stepped into Jerry's Men Shop. I admired my big brother as he picked out a dress shirt with matching pants, while saying they would look good on me. It felt great being with him as I followed him through the aisles of the store, knowing that I was cool. Even Lou, the owner's misfit brother-in-law, with his waistband pulled up just below his breast-line, knew that my brother had chutzpah, had it going on.

After getting the clothes, it was always across the street and into Nedick's for a much needed hot dog with an orangeade drink. I can still remember the smell and the taste of those things! It's funny how the senses, like smells, can evoke certain memories.

EIGHT

"What are you going to have, Steve?"

"I'll have the cheeseburger deluxe, medium-rare, with fried onions and a diet cola."

"How about you Dan?" asked out waitress.

"I'll have something soft and gooey."

"And what'll that be, Dan?"

"Oh, you know, with rye toast," he countered.

"Dan, I swear I don't know. Is that eggs?"

"What? I'm sorry, I didn't hear you," he said.

"Do you want eggs, Dan?"

"Oh, yeah, eggs," he said

"And how would you like your eggs cooked?"

"Ohhh, soft and gooey, please."

"Do you want coffee with that, Dan?" she asked.

"Yeah, I mean no… yeah, I'll have Sanka."

"Sanka?"

"Yes, Dan means decaf," I interrupted. "Sanka was from fifty years ago."

"Oh," said our waitress, as she scurried off to the kitchen.

"I'll be right back, Steven. I'm going out to have a ciggie," said Dan.

"I'll keep your coffee wet for you," I said.

Dan stood up while pushing off the table for balance. "You know, Steve, Uncle Harry smoked fifty cigarettes a day, and he's now ninety-five years old!"

It was the usual. My brother was driving the waitress crazy. Thank God they knew him and liked him. He was harmless, but what a pain in the ass he could be at times. He thought he was pretty funny, like an old- time Jewish borsht-belt comedian working in the Catskills.

He had the rhythm, but lacked all of the punch lines, which of itself was pretty funny. He usually made up something close to the actual punch line. Sometimes it was just a bunch of sounds like "hubba hubba hubba," which when said quickly sounds like Hebrew. This usually makes people laugh because it's absurd.

Upon leaving the diner, we noticed that the temperature had dropped at least by twenty degrees. This was mid-July, but it felt like fifty degrees. Once again, a fog had rolled in, thick and white. The sky turned dark and thundered. You could feel the air being sucked up, leaving a heavy blanket of humidity. What looked like lightning snaked across the sky, but it could not be heard. There was no rain, though. I turned on my high beams to cut through the smog and carefully trekked my way home.

Then the thunderous blasts started. The walls in my house shook and the neighborhood dogs began barking. The cable TV went off, and the lights went out. Waiting for the next thunder clap was unnerving. I stood outside on my front porch, just watching. My neighbors came out onto their own porches, staring at the sky. Dan stayed inside smoking, saying that it was too dangerous to stick our heads outside.

This was no ordinary storm. The thunder was ear-shattering, a blitzkrieg of monstrous bombs exploding, a freakish July Fourth celebration without the fanciful color displays. Jagged lines of broken dulled lights hung lazily above, suspended, a poor replication of lightening bolts. There was no rain, nor wind. It stopped after forty- five minutes. All that was left was the fog.

I went back into the house and Dan and I sat in the

den, hoping to see if there was anything on the news regarding the storm. Looking at him, I noticed a resemblance to Albert Einstein during his later years. Dan's hair was uncombed and wild. The middle part of his forehead had a huge piece of hair missing, giving him that pious-monk look. On his sides, it stuck out or stood straight up. Even so, he still managed to have more hair than I did. His beard was a picture of beauty as well, long and bushy. I don't know if it was due to the storm, but Dan looked as if his head had just come out of the dryer with a bad case of static cling.

He was now playing that old TV time game show with me, "The Sixty-four Thousand Dollar Question." The questions were really anything that Dan could think of as his mind wandered. They were really hard to answer. I didn't like to play. I always found myself being the losing, irritable contestant on his show.

Suddenly it began. "Steve, how much does it cost to open a diner in Greenwich Village?"

Most of these questions I ignored. How would I know and why would I care?

"Steve, did you ever read Antoine Duboise's *Into The Night*?"

"No, Dan, what's it about?"

"Oh, some of the injustices of the First World War!"

It was amazing, though. He could remember facts from years ago but had a hard time ordering his food. He could not grasp the concept of separating garbage from recyclables, or perhaps he was just too lax. He couldn't keep a clean apartment either. Yet, he could recall some obscure facts from his school days that I never knew if they were true or not. Most of the time that I doubted him, the information turned out to be correct. Often, I would find myself scurrying off to the dictionary, encyclopedia, or the computer to verify these things. At other times he would just make up things to see how gullible I was, testing his superior wisdom to mine. Some test! Nice Game Show! I was praying that there wouldn't be a bonus round.

"You know, Steve, only five percent of our land is lived on."

Uh-oh, I thought. Was this in the form of a question, or some kind of a trick? Were we now playing "Jeopardy?" At this point, I made a hasty retreat back to my sanctuary, my bedroom. Later in the evening, I heard my name called, "Steve, Steve, Steve." Was my mind playing tricks on me again? I rolled over in bed to see Dan standing by my bedroom door.

"Dan, what's up?" I asked?

"Steve, I wanted to tell you that Doctor Abukabar asked me to participate in a program with other people."

"Oh, yeah," I answered. "What for?"

"He said to talk to those voices that I've been hearing on the radio."

I let it sink in for a moment before I responded. "Get out of here!" I said. "What are you going to do?"

"Well, I don't want to travel anywhere, so I told him no."

"Good for you, Dan. You don't need to be doing that thing. It sounds kind of crazy to me."

NINE

"Anyway, President Smith, the experiment ended as a complete failure. No contacts were made."

"You mean to tell me, Neary, that none of these so-called clairvoyants could contact this thing? Then it's a hoax!"

"No, President Smith, we don't think that it is. We had these challenged people in the NOMAD Command Center in Nu Daz, New Mexico for five days straight. We tried all means possible for contact, yet nothing. But, for some reason, we do believe that these people are not part of a grand scheme."

"Therefore, Neary, what you're telling me is that this thing is real?"

Vivian Neary paced the President's office before answering.

"Jim," she said, "we believe that something is definitely going on. With the weather changes, eerie sightings, and voices, people are demanding some answers."

Jim peered down at his feet, shuffling them in place, perplexed.

"What answers, Neary?" he pleaded. "What should I do?"

"Something, Jim. You've got to say something," she said. President Smith was still wearing his silk pajamas and bathrobe, being woke early by Vivian's unexpected visit.

"Listen, Vivian, I don't want anything to leak out about this. Let's keep this a weather-related issue. I want you to do a release saying that it is weather-related, okay? Work this out with NASA, or NOMAD, but nothing to create a panic, or else those crazy terrorists will come out of the woodwork. Who knows what could happen in this crazy world we live in?"

The very next day, the nation read in their newspapers that weather service and NASA scientists were proclaiming strange weather conditions due to solar flares, along with the partial loss of the ozone layer. It was nothing to be concerned about. To the dismay of the President, though, pages one and two reported that certain Middle Eastern nations were pointing their fingers at Israel, accusing them of using some new form of weaponry to adversely affect the weather.

If it was not curtailed, Israel would face dire consequences. Terrorism was also feared to be possible throughout other parts of the world as well. Strict religious fanatics were inferring that the end was near. Many other countries were reporting the increase in citizens hearing voices and making contact with an entity of some sort. So far, this fact could not be officially verified.

Later that night, there was a knock on my door around eight o'clock. It was my next-door neighbor, Al.

"Hey, Al," I said. "What's going on?"

"Just come outside."

I went outside and looked at Al, thinking that he had something to tell me.

"Yeah, so what's up?" I asked.

Al said, "Look up."

As he motioned his fingers across the street, my eyes focused over my neighbors' roof. "Oh, man," I said. "I can see what you mean now."

Although the sky was pitch black for the most part,

there were faintly lit areas in irregular shapes, some in the form of lightning bolts. These were not moving, though. They were rigid.

"Holy cats," I said. "They're still there from last night. What in God's name do you think they are?"

"I don't know, Steve, but they said on TV that it's weather-related and has something to do with those sun spots, or sun bursts that we get in our atmosphere."

"C'mon, Al. I don't believe a word that there saying when they use that excuse for this. I mean, look at it. That's supposed to be caused by the sun?" I demanded.

TEN

The General Security Meeting of the United World of Nations came to order at eight-thirty in the morning. The meeting was called to ease increased hostile escalations and allegations from many countries worldwide. All nations were present. An agenda was set. Opening remarks by the General President of the UWN clearly stated that no country was behind the strange phenomena happening in the world. All attending nations would have a chance to address their concerns to the General Assembly.

Hostilities were expressed as expected in the morning session. The afternoon session had presentations from different scientists around the world. An evening meeting was set for the signing of an agreement to thwart any armed conflicts and to address all concerns to a de facto committee. Day two called for a coordinating committee to gather information from the scientific community in the days to come. Their job was to find out the true explanation for the recent phenomena. The primary concern of the General Assembly was to cool everyone's heels.

"Nobody is up to anything!"

Though true for all attending, little could be done to stop any religious fervor or the terrorist threats that had begun to fester. And word was getting out about the voices being heard.

Meanwhile, back in Washington, President Smith was finding himself trapped between a rock and a hard place. He rang his administrative assistant on the phone.

"Yes, President Smith?" he inquired.

"Pat, put me through to Nicolas Fungitto, our

Ambassador to the United World of Nations, please. Thanks."

"Nick, it's me, Jim Smith. Yes, Nick, how are you? Listen, I've just heard about the agendas set up at the UWN. What the hell is going on, Nick? Don't you know that I didn't want any publicity getting out about strange beings or aliens talking to people? What do they want to do, cause a riot? What do you mean you couldn't stop them? I told you to ask the General Assembly to keep a lid on this stuff. Well, now we're going to look like imbeciles and the American people are going to want answers and fast! Your job was to ask for a veto on that info. Oh, you couldn't get the majority vote, I see. What about England, they didn't back us up? Oh, come on, Nick! Okay, just forget about it. We'll do a press release tomorrow concocting some cockamamie story about this, Nick. Don't worry about it. I'll take care of it."

The very next day, the newspapers exploded with the stories. Page one was about the UWN meeting with its findings and agendas set forth. The President's press agents scripted almost the exact same storyline as the UWN's. His speech varied only by mentioning that all of his department heads were vigilantly working on these problems. He stressed that there was nothing to worry about and that he stood in total agreement with the United World of Nations. The notion of voices was casually swept under the rugs, for the time being.

ELEVEN

The Grand Cardinal Sephus, of the International Order of Holy Ministries, gave his weekly television sermon that following Sunday morning. It read as follows:

"The Ministries are concerned about the latest series of events which have affected all of the countries of the world. We are aware that our planet is going through changes due to mankind. We are calling for all nations to make a commitment toward taking better care of our planet. We also believe that some of the incredible phenomena witnessed and heard may be of the hand of the Lord showing His disdain. We are also aware of many people who have felt that they have been in the presence of a spirit during these times. Doctors and newspapers have been referring to a large number of these people as the challenged, imbalanced, or disoriented. We take offense to these types of labels. It is a time to pray and to ask our Lord for His service and His guidance."

TWELVE

July twenty-second was a beautiful day. Everyone was on the beach. Here, I met my good friend, Bryan, along with his daughter, Tristen. That is Bryan with a Y, and oh, what a ladies' man he is. Bryan was the type of guy all the ladies wanted. Although not tall, he gave the impression that he was. Perhaps not quite six feet, he was a good looking man, blond hair, pronounced nose, blue eyes and physically fit. I guess I admired his gift of gab most of all. He was never at a loss for words. Bryan could always think of something nice to say about any woman. For instance, if a hypothetical lady was only a nose lying on a beach blanket (and not even an attractive nose), Bryan would still find something nice about her to say.

"Your nose is tanning lovely."

"What a cute pimple that is."

"I'm sorry. I thought you were a model and that I saw that nose in a magazine somewhere."

Pitter-patter, their hearts would skip a beat. How did he do that? Bryan gave the impression that he was a concerned man, a very deep man and they loved that. He wanted them to feel desirable and, at the same time, as if they could speak to him about anything, the whole shebang! For Bryan was a great listener, as well.

Yes, I loved Bryan. Although we were different, we weren't opposites. Opposite was my other good buddy, Charlie. I put myself somewhere in the middle of them. Listening to Charlie was like hearing the wisdom of my dad again, very conservative and untrusting of the world around us. If I closed my eyes, I would think that some ninety-year-old Italian guy was talking to me. Oh, I loved that Charlie, too.

We set up our chairs and blankets and sat down.

"So, Bryan, how's it going? I asked.

"Not bad, Steve."

We had waited until Bryan's daughter went down to the water to talk.

"So, what do you think about all of this crazy stuff that's been happening?" I asked him.

"Well, it's definitely weird. Something's going on or going to happen. It seems, though, that everyone is trying to ignore it or play it down," he said.

"Bryan, have *you* heard any voices?"

"Only the crazy bitches trying to call me at all hours of the day, Steve."

And then he laughed.

"They won't leave me alone, especially the married ones."

And he laughed again.

"Bryan, I mean other voices, the kind that you think you hear in your head."

"No, Steve," he said. "Maybe you've been hanging around your brother too long, you know?"

"I know, Bryan, but I really mean it. It's not like I hear them in my head. It's more like someone is whispering over my shoulder, but there is nobody there. I've only heard them a couple of times, and it seems to be when I'm tired or almost falling asleep."

"You know," Bryan said with concern, "you'd better watch it, Steve. You're starting to scare me."

"Look, Bryan, I think that something is going to happen too, even though the newspapers are saying there is nothing to worry about. I know that Danny is hearing something. I know that his doctor really did call him and asked him to participate in some kind of experiment. You see, most people don't believe there are voices."

Bryan looked down at the water to check on his daughter.

"Listen," he said, "you can't deny the whacky weather we've been having lately. And I'll tell you something else. These women have been nuttier than ever, Steve."

I raised my body up to shake off some of the sand and then looked my buddy in the eyes.

"You've got to be careful," I said. "I've told you that before. Just go out with the single ones, will you? I keep thinking that one day I'll open up the newspaper to see that you've been shot by a jealous husband."

THIRTEEN

"Steve, Steve, Steve, can you hear me?"

"Yeah," I said, "what do you want?"

"I want to talk with you. Do you feel like you are dreaming right now?"

Yeah, I know that I'm dreaming. I'm not even moving my mouth, I thought.

"Well, you're not."

"Yeah, okay........"

"We're the voices, Steve. We're the voices that your brother has been hearing."

Oh, this is a good dream. I don't even have to talk in this dream, I thought.

"That's correct, Steve. You only have to think what you want to say, and I will respond. Better yet, don't even bother thinking. I will know your next question and will answer it."

Oh, this is a weird dream that I'm having.

"I am talking to you because I have decided to start talking to others aside from the challenged folks like your brother. Does that answer your question, Steve? In answer to your next question, we or I began with the challenged, because they're accustomed to hearing voices in the first place and are easily accessible. It's our way of causing less chaos and disruption to your planet."

Okay, I thought. *I'm not liking this dream anymore. I'm going to get up now.*

"Steve, I don't think that is possible. Try opening your eyes now. Did you open them? Do you see your bedroom? Turn on your light if you'd like? Are you okay, Steve? We can talk this way, or anyway that you please"

"Yeah, I think so," I said dumbfounded, as I opened up my eyes. I sat up in my bed and turned on my lamp. I jumped out of bed when I heard that voice again.

It said, "Are you all right now, Steve?"

"Holy cow," I responded out loud. "Yes, I think that I'm all right."

"Okay, good," said the voice, satisfied. I waited to see if it spoke again.

"I'm going to let you really go to sleep now and dream about something in your past that you'll like. Something about your childhood, your brother, the love that you share. Can you handle that?" asked the entity.

"Yeah," I whispered, frightened and feeling a chill as I stood in the dark. "I think that I can. As long as you don't give me a heart attack."

I got back in bed, fell asleep and dreamed.

FOURTEEN

"Hey, we were here first," I said.

"Get off the field, kid," said the bigger guy, "or I'll beat the living crap out of you!"

Just then, the older kid pushed me down to the ground. There was one swift kick that he administered under my left thigh as I fell sideways into the fetal position. The schoolyard concrete was hard and jagged on my hands as I tried to push myself up. At that very instant, a blurred object slammed into him while he was still straddling me. It was Dan, who had come from the other side of the schoolyard where he was playing in his own game of box baseball with his friends. They started spinning around as if caught in each other's orbit.

The kids in the schoolyard quickly gathered around screaming and yelling, choosing sides for their friend, although this kid was way outnumbered. He was Edgar Abramowitz, the same age as Dan. Perhaps he had three guys rooting for him. Meanwhile, my brother had nearly twenty of his friends calling him on by his nickname, "Moose."

"Come on, Big Moose", "Hit him good, slam him down", "Come on Danny, Danny, Danny!"

My brother was nicknamed Moose after Bill "Moose" Skowron, first baseman of the New York Yankees, since Dan played first base in the schoolyard. I was known as "Little Moose," simply because I was his little brother. Everybody in the schoolyard had a nickname. It was a kid's God-given right to have one, to demand one, after acceptance into the schoolyard.

Dan was pummeling Edgar now, even though Edgar outweighed my brother by a good thirty pounds. I was getting into it louder than the others, since I wanted to see Edgar's blubber distilled for his assault on me.

"Come on Dan, kick his butt!" I screamed.

My brother was now getting the upper hand, as he was pushing him around pretty good and slugging him with the unexpected left hand. My brother was a lefty, and if a kid's not used to the left, then he's in for a surprise. Fat boys tend to tire quicker, too, and such was the case with Edgar, as his legs were weighing heavy and his breath was growing shorter. At this point of my ecstasy, a sudden weight slammed onto my back. I could hear the onlookers roar much louder as Edgar's younger brother Sheldon could no longer witness his brother's beating and decided to go after me. Sheldon surprised me, as he was just a smaller version of his fat brother.

When I realized who was on my back, I got into one of those adrenaline rushes. The onlookers were now delirious as this fight turned into a double-header, two fights for the price of one, a brother tag-team match. It doesn't get much better than that in the Bronx! It was the infamous Shapiros versus the Abramowitzs match and it went down into city folklore, etched in time forever. There is an old saying, "to see red." And it's a true saying. One must have experienced it firsthand to know that it actually exists. At that moment, perhaps for the first time in my life, I saw red, quite literally, as blood rushed through my eyes and somehow creates a red glare. Perhaps the adrenaline and the endorphins kicked in?

Whatever the case, my ears we're ringing from the volume of blood that rushed towards my brain. The red was like a curtain that comes down over the eyes;

end of scene one, stage left. The audience was allowed to see the aggression and acts of violence that were administered on the other side of this curtain. At this point in the play I became a madman! My strength was multiplied by the square root of pi. With Sheldon on my back, I performed my patented spin-o-rama move, knowing that one of us was bound to get dizzy and fall down. I felt like I had lifted a baby grand piano all by myself, as we spun towards the giant fifteen-foot schoolyard fence.

I was thinking on my feet. I knew that I had to slam Sheldon into the fence. Over and over we spun until we reached it. Finally, with the destination nearing, I caught him real good as I turned him with the precision of a Mikhail Baryshnikov move on the dance floor into that chain-linked monster.

To my dismay, he didn't fall down but instead landed on his feet, groggy. By then I didn't care as my blind fury took over, and I began to whale on him, arms flailing windmill style, without thinking, like the mad Russian that I was. From the corner of my eye, I could see that Danny had Edgar against the fence too, striking him one blow after the other. My brother was always there for me as we took a unanimous victory on that glorious day under the shadows of Yankee Stadium in the Bronx. And, I thought to myself, subconsciously, *could this be the nice dream that I was promised*?

FIFTEEN

"What a dream! I can't believe you haven't spoken to that voice yet," I told Bryan as we drove down to Atlantic City for one of our nights out at a casino club. I could see that Bryan was now questioning my mental health.

"I swear! I dreamed it!" I insisted.

"Well, tell me something, Steve. If this happened last night to a lot of people, why wasn't it on the news this morning?"

I was keeping my eyes on the road while doing seventy and found his disbelief in me annoying.

"Look," I said, "maybe he's picking those that he speaks to now? And why would it be on the news today? He's been speaking to open-minded people only."

Bryan stared at me indignantly, with his bloodshot eyes wide open and that Tupperware thirty-ounce jug-a-lug spilling his homemade triple shot rum and coke onto my carpet.

"So, Steve, you don't think that you were just dreaming?"

"No, I swear. I woke up and spoke with him," I said.

"Come on, Steve, what makes you think that you're more open-minded than me? Get off your high horse."

Bryan took another swig of his rum, while losing some of it from the side of his mouth. His eyes swelled larger than two red moons.

"Well," I said, "I think that it's because of your religious views."

"What" he spat. "My religious views?" He laughed out loud.

"Yeah," I said. "I think that because you're a

born-again Christian, you're not open-minded enough. You're too close-minded."

Bryan stared at me contemptuously.

"Oh, come on," he countered, "that's just a lot of crap!"

We drove the rest of the way in dead silence until we hit the parking garage of the casino. There, we opened a couple of beers and drank in the car while we spoke again. Then, we left the parking lot and headed for the club, feeling much better.

No sooner had we entered, than Bryan was on the dance floor with a hot number and was applying his patented dip move. This lady was definitely digging it, although the initial look of fear was still present on her face. *Oh, boy,* I thought, *here comes the "I will pick you up in my arms and sway you like a baby move."* And then it came, astonishing the onlookers. Other dancers stared in disbelief while the bouncers wondered if they should remove him. I do believe, though, that other female bystanders were wishing they were in her place.

"Oh, what a feeling, to be held like a baby again," thought this lady. *"I think this might be the man for me."*

Bryan lifted and turned her like a rag doll, and then followed with a nifty tango step.

"Perhaps, my ship has finally come in," she thought. *"Where has this hunk been all of my life? Maybe I'll divorce that no good for nothing husband I live with."* She was really letting herself get carried away.

"Oh--oh, don't do it, Bryan," I said to myself. I could tell it was coming. It was the "I'll–swing-you-between-my-legs" move. As this lady now experienced weightlessness again in her life, her mini skirt hitched up above her thighs, eliciting an even louder gasp from those watching, and the imaginary judges' cards

flashed up, reading nine, nine point-five, and a nine for the scores. The band kept on playing, riveted by Bryan's moves, while his newfound dance partner screamed "Oh, my God!" as the spin cycle started. I could faintly hear her say, "What's your name again? Is that Bryan with a Y?" as they came off of the dance floor, holding hands and nestled together.

"Yes, it is," Bryan replied in her ear, in his macho baritone. "And did you know that you are the most beautiful woman here tonight? Can I buy you a drink?"

SIXTEEN

"So, what's with the President?" Press Secretary Scott Knowles asked Vivian Neary, as they walked down the corridor to the President's Oval Office.

"You see, Scott, he's all screwed up over this dream crap. He asked me to bring you in on this matter so that you can do a press release for tomorrow. Just remember, he's having a very hard time with this, so just go easy with the guy," she asked, while standing outside of the door. She knocked on the door and then entered with Scott.

"Jim, I brought Scott as you asked."

"Scott, sorry to drag you in on this so late in the evening. We met all day with our Joint Chiefs of Staff, and we have to do a release for tomorrow's news. Look, this stuff is going to hit the fan. We want to get in on it first. Scott, I honestly don't know what to think about all of this crap. Some of my staff is telling me that they have dreamed this stuff, too. I have not, so half of me says that you're all crazy, but I have to protect my image. You know the routine. Have the minutes from the meeting changed to mirror what the press releases. Contact your man. As for me, tell the public that there is nothing to fear. All matters are being reviewed by the Administration."

SEVENTEEN

"Hey, how are you, beautiful? I loved the photos that you e-mailed me. You look great! So, what do you think? We get together for some drinks this Friday?"

"Bryan, I need to talk with you."

"Well, go ahead, Karen. I'm all ears. You e-mailed me to call you."

"Bryan, this is not Karen,"

"Oh, no, don't tell me that I've called the wrong person again?"

"No, Bryan. In fact, I think that you are talking to the right person."

"What do you mean by that? Who is this?"

"Bryan, I don't have a name. But you can call me by any name that you wish."

"Okay, Steve, I know this is you. This is a good one. How are you doing the girl's voice?"

"It's not Steve."

"Yeah, right. Okay, you're starting to scare me now. I see, Steve! You're trying to make me think that I'm being contacted by that thing. Good one, Steve!"

"You are Bryan with a Y."

"All right, I'm getting off the phone now. This is not funny anymore."

"That would not be wise, Bryan. I'm giving you the chance of a lifetime, and you do know that eventually, I will talk to you."

"All right, show me that this is not Steve. Tell me something that only I know?"

"Okay, Bryan, how about that your mom's maiden name is McClaratty, and that your real first name is Rudolf. Bryan, are you still there?"

"Yes, so you mean that I'm really being contacted?"

"Yes, you are."

"But, how come you're a woman?"

"I'm whatever you'd like to think that I am, Bryan."

"I only thought that you spoke to people on the TV, radio, or in their sleep?

"Oh, come on, Bryan, grow up! I can contact people in many ways. Believe me, this is the best way for you. Later, we can use different forms of contact, which I understand you are an expert at."

"Well, that is true," Bryan said, as he chuckled confidently.

"See, Bryan, we can get along. I promise you that we'll have some of the best talks of your life. In fact, life is what I'm here to talk to you about tonight. Let me get to the most important part of our discussion, Bryan, which is sex. We can talk about anything, but let's start there," said the entity.

"Okay, so you want to help me with my sex life?"

"Yes, I do. You know, Bryan, you're not the only one that needs to have a sex talk. You see, your world is in a pretty bad way with this sex thing. Humans can't seem to figure out sex from love. Total confusion here."

"I can't believe that I'm talking to you. I really don't know what to call you? Are you God, or is this a joke?" asked Bryan.

"No, Bryan, I'm certainly not God and in no way should this reflect on your way of belief. I am another living thing, just as you, but very different from you. Let's save this God stuff for another day. Here is what I suggest. Since you have to work tomorrow, why don't we continue this conversation in your sleep, your dream state? How's that sound to you?"

"Fine, I guess?"

"Great, then. You'll see that we will cover much

more ground this way, and it will seem like a movie to you. I promise that I will not scare you. Is that okay?"

"Yeah, let's go for it," replied Bryan.

EIGHTEEN

"We are such stuff as dreams are made on,
and our little life is rounded with sleep"

William Shakespeare, The Tempest

"Bryan, just relax. Mankind is not in harmony. The hands that you touch in life affect the hands of all nations, races, religions and people of this world. Mankind has evolved into a competitive dog eat dog society."

"What has that got to do with sex, though?" asked Bryan.

"Plenty," replied the entity. The tensions that you create with your mate extend to the tensions all around us. From couples, to family, to people, to nations, tensions are formed from hypocrisy and dishonesty. Your world has become a hot bed of these. Your Bibles preach goodness, yet why are there religious wars? Why is killing all other creatures acceptable for mankind in the eyes of God? The Bible promotes love for procreation, not for sex! Meaningless sex would be acceptable if it didn't ruin and hurt relationships of two people, then hurt families and those around them and upward throughout the world. It's a chain of events and feelings that shape your world. You're all too busy rushing through life to see this. 'Get out of my way, I want to have an affair with your wife, I'm not happy with mine!' This is your mindset, Bryan."

"Dreams, Bryan, are closer to reality than you can imagine. Your mind works while you are asleep. Your dreams tap into the portal to your soul. Rest easy now. Let everything go..."

Bryan found himself looking at the eve of creation. There was an abundance of nature, overflowing with lush forestry and flowery scents. There was a pond in the shape of a heart. There were maidens bare, bringing forth wines and delicacies. He could feel his own heart beating slower and his breathing becoming deeper. The smells of lilacs and fragrances drifted, filling his head with emotions. He was mesmerized, dreamlike, floating above this pond. He was outside of his body, above it, staring below at his clothes, which lay crumpled on the ground. He wanted to say something, to express himself, but his mouth was parched, unmoving.

"Bryan," the voice said, "does it feel like love, or sex?"

He heard the voice from inside of himself. He couldn't respond.

NINETEEN

It may have been July twenty-fourth, or the twenty-fifth, but it didn't really matter which. That morning I picked up the newspaper at the local convenience store where there was a crowd of people milling about and talking outside. They were all talking about an alien thing that some had had contact with. I heard such things as, "I think I'm going crazy" and then, "That hasn't happened to *me*, man!" *It's finally hitting home*, I thought. *Half of the world has been speaking to this unknown voice while the other half has not.*

The headlines read, "WORLD IS CONTACTED or is it Mental Madness?" Another read, "HOAX or REAL?" One of the guys in front of the store asked me whether I had spoken to it. I hesitated at first to answer, but then thought what the heck and said yes. Two other guys immediately chimed in, saying, "See, I told you so." The others stood perplexed. "Oh, so you're another nut," I heard the only female present say.

When I arrived back at home, I flipped on the TV. Every channel was talking about the headlines, whether it was a talk show or a news show. All sorts were being interviewed, from politicians to the random man on the street. The consensus was that it had to be true and that the rest of the world would be contacted soon.

It was quite different on the international level, though. Certain nations were pointing fingers at archenemies, accusing them of orchestrating these headlines in order to create chaos and disorder. Reprisals, they said, would be forthcoming if these fabrications persisted. Still other countries were exhorting a different viewpoint. They maintained that these voices were a sign from God and that the end was drawing near. "You will face your Maker, and if you are not of His persuasion, your time will end." Regardless of viewpoints, the world was showing itself to be in turmoil upon its first possible alien contact. Who would have guessed?

TWENTY

President Smith was beside himself. "Why not me?" he'd ranted since he awoke. He was getting a head count of all staff, cabinet members, as well as congressional legislators that had heard the voices. In front of his mirror adjusting his tie, he stood only five foot six inches tall. Never much in stature, he found other ways to make up for this shortcoming through cunning. He had a way with words, not that he could beat anyone in a debate, but he would manage in an "I told you so" type of ridicule. He was thin and lean for his age of fifty-nine, though.

"What am I," he asked, "some kind of loser, some kind of idiot that doesn't deserve to be contacted? Oh, I see, I'm not open-minded enough to be contacted? I wouldn't believe all of this stuff if you guys weren't telling me this. Go on, I want to hear it again from each and everyone of you, of how you got contacted. Come on, what was it like? Please, fill me in."

Press Secretary Knowles spoke.

"Look, Jim, it's nothing on you or anyone else not spoken to. It's definitely not a hoax since it's happened to so many people. Look, who knows what this really is? It's the unknown right now, and that's the scary part of it. But if this is the real thing, then this is a monumental time for mankind and we will be on top of this."

"That's what I like to hear, Scott," responded the President.

"Jim, Doctor Chekaras out at the NOMAD has been conducting and evaluating tests on our servicemen who say that they were contacted. His test results are proof positive that they are not lying. It's interesting that all contacts are made away from the base, never on military grounds, though, Jim."

"So, Scott, this thing is purposely staying away from certain people and places, I take it," said President Smith.

"Seems that way, Jim. We cannot contact the thing from the NOMAD Command center. Another item of interest is that it can only be heard and not seen."

"So, where is this thing? Where is it coming from?" demanded Jim. Scott shook his head in dismay.

"We can't pick anything up on radar or any telescopes. We don't know. It seems to only converse with people one-on-one and sometimes through dreams. So we're really stumped! It talks about the blight in the world."

"Well, then, why the hell can't I speak with it?" asked Jim.

Scott held his tongue for a second.

"In due time," he said. "All in due time, Jim."

TWENTY-ONE

"It spoke to me, Steve. I can't believe it."

"Good for you, Bryan," I said.

Bryan and I were sitting on the beach again, enjoying a perfect day. His daughter Tristen was body surfing.

"At first, I thought it was you, Steve, playing games with me."

"No, it wasn't me," I said.

"Then the thing started talking to me, you know, a normal conversation."

"Listen, Bryan," I said, "I'm starting to worry about you. Maybe you need professional help?"

"What, are you kidding me?" he asked.

"Yes, I'm just getting even with you for not believing me when it happened to me, you big idiot. I couldn't help myself," I said as I chuckled.

"Oh, okay."

Bryan composed himself.

"So this thing talked to me about sex. Can you believe it?" he said. "Of all people, he spoke to me!"

"Couldn't have picked a better person for the job," I replied.

"Yeah, you're right about that. But it made perfect sense to me, too."

"Well, I'm glad someone finally got through to you."

"Listen, Steve, I was scared to death at first. I didn't know what was happening. Then it said I should go to bed and that it would speak to me in my sleep. Like, what choice did I have? I thought I was going crazy. Listen, Steve. This thing made me dream about the feeling of love."

"Maybe it's trying to tell you something, Bryan, you know?"

"Yeah, I think so."

"Well, look," I said. "You really should feel honored that it spoke with you. A lot of people..."

I just stopped my thought in mid-sentence as I looked at my shoulder.

"What the hell is this?" I said. "Is that rain coming down or snow?"

"I just had a snowdrop fall on my shoulder," said Bryan. "I think it's snow, Steve. What the heck is going on?"

We both looked up to the sky and could see individual snowflakes dropping as if it were winter. The temperature felt about ten degrees cooler. Then the snow fell down in sheets in a matter of seconds.

"This is crazy, man," I told Bryan.

As I spoke, Bryan stood up quickly and ran down to the water to find Tristen. I got up and followed behind. We couldn't see thirty feet in front of us as the ocean was obscured by a July blizzard. Bryan was holding Tristen by the shoulders, while large crowds were now standing with us by the ocean's edge, talking about this strange occurrence. It was a spring snow shower in July.

"This is crazy," I repeated.

"You know, Steve, I think that it's trying to make believers out of everyone," Bryan replied.

"I agree with you, buddy, but do you think that it is causing all of these strange conditions, too?" I asked.

As quickly as it began, it cleared up again, lending the appearance of a fresh spring day. People were returning to their blankets, sitting back down while nervously chatting to one another. The sun peeked out brightly while warming back up to July standards. The snow melted away as if it was a desert mirage, dreamlike with its transience. Bryan, Tristen, and I returned to our blanket while scanning the beach around us. We gradually settled down, Bryan and I into our chairs and Tristen onto the blanket. I was facing the ocean, while they faced me. Tristen held her hand up against the glare of the sun, as Bryan reached for their sunglasses. It seemed as if half of the sunbathers had left in an awful hurry. No doubt the sudden snow had scared the wits out of everyone.

The beachgoers that remained were talking about witnessing such a strange phenomenon. Bryan started to tell me again how the voice sounded, as if it was a whisper from behind him.

"You know, I agree," I said. "At first, I thought it was someone behind me, too, and not my imagination.

"Yep, me, too," said Bryan. "It was almost like having the radio on playing softly behind me."

I was ready to tell Bryan a bit more about the voice when I stopped in mid-sentence. Instead, I stared intensely over his shoulder, facing the water. I squinted again and again, rubbing my eyes to be certain of what I was seeing. Reaching over for my eyeglasses, I nearly lost my balance but stopped my fall with the palm of my hand. I gingerly raised myself from my chair and tried to stand up. At this point in time, Bryan was looking at me, quite bewildered.

"What's up?" he asked.

I found it hard to gain my balance in the sand as I stumbled at first, finding my knees weak. I heard his question, but it faded to dissonance, like when a dentist is speaking to you, just as the sodium pentothal takes effect. My ears were buzzing. I didn't answer. Blood rushed in my head, and time seemed to slow. The very first screams were echoing now from other beachgoers. Many stood up and scanned the horizon. Bryan and Tristen sensed the urgency and were rising and turning in one motion toward the water.

I do believe that Bryan and I both uttered "Oh, God" at the same time, while Tristen screamed. There it was, right before our very eyes and from the makings of it, it was a whale. And a very huge whale at that! It must have been at least two hundred yards out in the surf. It seemed much closer than that due to its enormous size. This majestic creature was staring at us. Its eyes and forehead above the waterline, it measured a good twenty feet in girth. It was not moving though, only wavering ever so slightly in the ocean swell.

In the twelve to fifteen feet of water, the behemoth swayed gently like a ship from starboard to portside. His color was that of an elephant, a dark sandy grey, almost blue. It hovered there like a spacecraft, as if trying to get our attention. The stare down went on for a good twenty minutes, which felt like a lifetime. Beachgoers were no longer screaming but jabbering with each other about the amazing events unfolding. The lifeguards were advising us not to go into the water, although I couldn't imagine why anyone would.

I had never seen such a sight in my life nor had witnessed such behavior as this. Just as startling was the shriek let out by this gentle giant, sending everyone backwards by a good two feet. A huge spout of water shot out from his blowhole and sprayed us with a cooling mist borne in a breeze that seemed to come from nowhere. The winds picked up as the whale slowly navigated its bulk around in a one hundred-and-eighty-degree maneuver, allowing us a broad view of its flank, then meandering its way back out to sea.

TWENTY-TWO

President Smith was pacing the Oval Conference Room. All his staff was present for the emergency meeting he had called. The President spoke first.

"We have to do something, but what?"

Secretary of State Neary was first to respond.

"Jim, Doctor Lewis and I have an idea."

"Well, come on, Vivian, let me hear it."

"Jim, since this thing will not talk with our command center, military affiliates, or any government entity, we thought that perhaps we should ask the physicists and astronomers of our nation to try and speak for us. They meet under the auspice of the World Board of Physics and Astronomy, Jim. Many of them have reported speaking to this thing on a regular basis."

Jim removed his eyeglasses and cleaned them with his handkerchief. He cleared his throat.

"Don't you think that this thing, this entity, will know what we're doing? It seems to read minds, doesn't it?" he questioned.

"Yeah, that's quite possible Jim, but what do we have to lose?"

"All right, then. Can we use these people as a springboard to have them ask all of our questions?" Jim asked.

"I don't see why not, Jim," replied Vivian.

"Then what are we waiting for?"

"Let's try to push the envelope on this idea."

Three days later, Doctor Hideki Yokomachi was presiding over the emergency session of the World Board of Physics and Astronomy. Headphones were in use as the language translation decoder was broadcasting for all present.

"We have been asked by many nations of the world

to act as an intermediary and to speak with our visitor for them. As you know, this entity will not speak with certain people, those including the military, government officials, as well as the close-minded." This last statement brought about a chorus of laughs from the attendees.

"Excuse me, ladies and gentlemen, excuse me please! I know that it may sound trite to you, but with all due respect, this is an issue of worldly importance. It is a fact that our visitor has indeed told many of us this. Due to this dilemma we have agreed to act as an intermediary for many nations of the world. We are therefore asking for your assistance in this capacity. You must cooperate by speaking to the entity as you have done in the past, one on one. We know that our guest speaks only to one person at a time. We are also aware that recordings of prior conversations have not been possible. Therefore, we implore you to operate under this same assumption of no recording of conversations. We must maintain an amicable relationship with the entity, by all means. As we say universally, do not piss it off! Therefore, future conversations will be written down. We will also try to ask it questions that our national hosts are ardently concerned about, which are security related," he paused, then continued.

"We believe that the entity is friendly with peaceful intentions. We know from our past experience that we are able to speak frankly about anything and everything with it. Therefore, be forthright in all future contact. The entity seems to have the ability to read our minds and to be everywhere, listening. We will compare our notes at a later date."

TWENTY-THREE

"So, Doctor Chekaras, how did the World Board meeting go?"

"Very well, Jim. They are in total agreement regarding our contact for national security purposes."

"Good, Norman, good! Now how about you contacting this thing so that we can speak to it just like the rest of your cronies?"

"Well, Jim, I wish it was that easy. I've been trying, but it probably knows that I work with you, no insult intended."

"All right, Norman, keep trying and let me know if anything happens."

Later that night at ten, Doctor Chekaras did receive his wake-up call. He was watching the nightly news while dozing off.

"Norman… Norman… oh Norman, wake up!"

"Holy crap, what's that?" he exclaimed, sitting upright in his chair.

"Come on, Norman, you've been asking for me, haven't you?"

"Oh, my God, wait a minute; let me turn off the TV."

"No, Norman, keep it on. Your wife might think that you're crazy if she walks in and hears you talking to yourself. Just keep it on. I promise that you won't miss a thing."

"Okay, okay, hold on one minute."

"There. Are you comfortable, Norman?"

"Yes, I can't believe that you're finally talking to me. This is great."

"Well, the same here, Norm. I wanted to talk to you before and I would have, but your position in the government held me back. You see, Norman, you are a physicist, and you do have a greater capacity to understand that this is actually happening. That is why I am speaking to people like you first. My visit and how I go about it is calculated so that it causes the least amount of chaos or disruption. Believe me, Norman, your world can easily be set into chaos. It seems to be a natural human response. Everyone will be spoken to in due time."

"Listen, I don't know how to address you?"

"That's all right, Norm. Your mere consciousness will be enough for me. Just speak to me, or better yet, just think whatever you want. I can converse with you mentally, or verbally. Okay, Norm, then verbally it shall be!"

"I don't know where to start. How can I contact you in the future?"

"Norman, you can try to speak to me whenever you desire, but I will determine when. I can hear you all the time and speak with you at anytime that I wish. I'd rather choose the times, though! Let us say that I will know when it is advantageous to speak. I also know that you're thinking that I am God right now, but really, I'm not. Believe me, I'm a living creature like you are, Norman. I may be more advanced and not that ordinary, but that does not make me God! I choose my times to speak because people have the propensity to act irrationally if I don't."

"Are you peaceful, entity?"

"Yes, I am."

"And can you see into the future?"

"I know the past, the present, and the future, Norman."

"So, let me know about the future?"

"I'm sorry, Norman. That would be impossible to

do for reasons beyond your understanding. Please tell your President that he has nothing to fear. My intentions are peaceful. I visit to give knowledge. My journeys are far and wide and never-ending. Although alive and real, I am vastly different that you."

TWENTY-FOUR

Exhausted from the epic beach spectacle, I stretched out on my couch and turned on the television.

"Welcome to the Evening News July twenty-sixth. President Smith held his news briefing earlier in the day and acknowledged that all national security measures were being taken in regard to our safety in light of a possible alien contact. He went on to say that not all people have been contacted, including himself. These so-called alien voices have shown peaceful intentions. The nation should go about its business as usual. At this time, a Code Yellow has been placed in effect as a precautionary measure for possible terrorist acts.

In other news, the United World of Nations has issued a proclamation asking for all countries of the world to remain calm in light of these events. Scientists around the world are attempting to provide substantiated proof of these voices. Doctor Norman Chekaras, the President's Chief Advisor of the NOMAD Command Center in Nu Daz, New Mexico, has commented that test results from actual people contacted have in fact been validated.

In other parts of the world, more violence has escalated in the Middle East, parts of Malaysia, and other third world nations due to these voices. General President Ian Clancy of the United World of Nations has asked for peace amongst neighbors. The violence is retaliatory for suspected staged phenomena set up by neighboring countries, according to unnamed terrorists. The Grand Cardinal Sephus of the Holy Order has asked for an end to this violence. He has said that these contacts have brought out fears in one another's faith. This must stop as God sees only equals, no rivals. If this alien is in fact real, it does not want us to kill each other in vain. It is not a savior of one faith or another."

TWENTY-FIVE

"All right, Dan, we've got to go! And you should come with me. Katie, could I have my diet cola, please?"

"What about my drugs?" my brother asked me, as he fiddled with his pack of cigarettes.

"You have enough meds to last you two weeks, don't you?" I asked. "I mean, if worse comes to worse, you could always get a refill anywhere that we are going. Plus, we'll be gone for less than two weeks, and what are you going to do all alone at home without me? No diner, no transportation, no company, no Oogie! I'm taking him with me. I wouldn't go without him. Above all, we'll finally make that diner trip we've been planning for the last ten years! Can you imagine that, two stops a day at the diner of your choice? All the coffee and cigarettes you want. We'll even sit there for a maximum limit of two hours at each diner. How's that?" I asked.

"Oh, you've got this all planned out already, don't you, Hitler?" he said.

"Yeah, Dan, I do. And listen, cigarettes are cheaper down there in West Virginia. Think of how many cartons we can pick up!"

"Well, I don't know," he said, while nervously glancing at his smokes and tapping his fingers on the table.

"Look, brother, I always make it a point to stop at at least two diners a day whenever I'm traveling. It's always the highlight of my trips. You know, it's a taste of America! We'll eat our way through the country. You live for the diner."

"I don't know," said Dan. "I got to go smoke a

cigarette. This is too much to worry about. I like it at home. How am I going to pee all the time while we're traveling? You know that I have to go every five minutes."

"I'll bring the pee container along, Dan… you know, the empty laundry detergent container. You can sit in the back of the van at the table smoking, eating, drinking, writing poetry and peeing. What else can be better?"

"Let me think about it, Steve. It's too much pressure right now," he said.

Katie brought my cola to the table. I thanked her. She was leaving when Dan called out to her.

"Waitress, waitress, can I have some more Sanka?"

"Sure, Dan," she replied.

"Thanks, Elaine," he responded.

"Dan, it's Katie," I pointed out.

"Yeah, Katie, right. I got to have my smoke," he said. Dan was more subdued after his smoke. Katie brought our lunch.

"Roasted chicken for you, Dan. Cheeseburger as usual for you, Steve."

"Could I have a glass of water, Ellen?" he asked.

"Dan, it's Kate," I pointed out once more.

One final attempt to convince him on our ride home from the diner and I was done.

"Dan, we'll stay in motels every night, as long as you help me pay for it. I'll be able to do the Antique Trails Festival along the way. I'll bring the tent along in case we camp out one night. You can sleep in the van. Oh, yeah, the biggest reason that I think we should get away is because I'm afraid that some nut will probably try to attack the local nuclear power plant due to these terrorist threats. Why don't you say we get out of here for the time being?"

I could see that my last remark had a notable effect on my brother.

"Yeah, a terrorist threat. That's right," I repeated. Something else to worry about, I figured, especially since I'd be far away from here and he'd be stuck all by himself.

I hated to try to appeal to his fear by painting the worst scenario possible but I was at my wit's end. I could see the look of anxiety appear as a frown upon his face. My brother suggested that he would check with his doctor if it would be okay to go.

TWENTY-SIX

Oogie always knew that loading the van was a prelude to traveling. So, on this day, he was ecstatic seeing me running around berserk, with boxes into the van. Then again, he was ecstatic leaving on a trip, as well as, returning home from one. He seemed to be happy whether coming or going.

Loading the van prior to a trip was always a frustrating chore for me, though it was a futile gesture. I had to make lots of decisions and it always seemed to end up taking much longer than necessary. What to take with us? I desired the least number of clothes and items. I must have spent two hours shuffling things in and out of the van, rethinking what to take. I was mentally draining myself. Blankets, pillows, meds, CDs, tent, dog supplies, and a minimum of snacks in the cooler. *I think we have it.* But I wasn't quite sure. This went on for most of the morning. Eventually, I just gave up and took whatever was already loaded into the van, since I had to wake Dan up at noon.

I went back into the house and took out my saxophone to practice the blues scale before we left on our trip. I knew from experience that this was a surefire way of getting him up.

I heard him stirring, so I peeked my head into his apartment.

"Come on, Dan, we've got to go," I said. He didn't move.

"Come on, Dan, it's almost twelve-thirty."

Dan finally agreed to get up if we had lunch once again at the Riverside Diner, our diner of choice. It's funny how a place gets a name. There is no river within two miles of the place. The closest it was to a river was the car wash that it was prior to being converted to its diner status. Perhaps it should have been named " the Soup and Suds Place. We finished our meal and bid farewell to our comrades amid "good lucks," "see you soon," "don't forget to write," "bring us back something good," "hasta luego," "take care fellas," "take the high road," "don't let the flies get in your underwear," "don't forget about us" and "don't eat poison."

We were on our way and it was still the same day. We were making good time, as it was only about three in the afternoon. I told Dan that I would drive for as long as I could and then get a motel room no later than ten. Seven hours later and three hundred and twenty miles down the road, I pulled into a thirty-three-dollar-a-night Travelers Best Motel off of Route 80 in Virginia. The very first thing that Dan did was to go get two packs of Camels at the adjacent Piggly Wiggly.

TWENTY-SEVEN

Molly was clearing up the dishes on the counter at the Ashton Diner, our first diner stop. We had already checked into our dive at the Travelers Best. It was just what I wanted and just what I expected. "Can't beat it, stop here, clean bed-sheets." Thank God for those clean bed-sheets. $29.99 daily. I mean nothing against Ashton, Virginia, clean sheets, cheap cigs, a grizzly diner next to the motel right off of the exit. What else could one ask for?

We were finishing up our third cup of decaffeinated coffee after eating some good ole home-style greasy meatloaf and greens.

"Listen, Dan, I've been meaning to tell you, I really want to thank you for coming. I was really worried about staying at home with the power plant right next door. Call me a worrywart, but I get scared thinking about that terrorism stuff! What do you think, Dan?"

"Steve, I think that half of the world is handling this thing well, but the other half is not. I guess that I'm a little apprehensive no matter where I go or what I do. I didn't want to stay home alone after you told me that. I just want my meds, smokes, and a pot to pee in."

"Have you been speaking to the entity lately?" I asked him.

"Yeah, all of the time, everyday."

"But I don't see you talking to him," I said.

"I do talk to him, but it's all mental now. It's like the other voices in my head. I speak to him all of the time," said my brother.

"But," I asked, "how can you tell if it's him and not the other voices in your head?"

"That's easy. He has a distinct voice, and he always refers to me by my name. He's much more gentle than those other voices that sound like static and make my mind race," said my brother.

Just then our waitress returned and asked us if we were having anything else.

"No, Molly," I replied.

"Well, I'll take that check for you, and don't forget to come on back," she said. "Yeah, we'll see you. Let's go, Dan. Three bucks is fine to leave her."

TWENTY-EIGHT

"So, what's eating you, Dan?"

"Oh, I'm obsessed about life and death."

"Well, so is everyone, Dan. That is a human thing. What is it that gets to you?"

"That you've got to die! That life is too short."

"I can imagine that it must be quite worrisome, Dan."

"Oh, it is. I spend most of my time thinking about it. My uncle Harry is ninety- six, and he stopped smoking ten years ago. My uncle Jack lived to be one hundred."

"So, what does that mean to you, Dan?"

"It means that maybe I'll live another thirty years or more. I know that Steve acts as if he doesn't care about dying, but he does."

"It must be a horrible thought to know that your life will end, Dan. I have no idea what that must feel like. In fact, I'm obsessed with the fact that I have to live forever. We have no records dating back to our beginning, Dan. We can see no end, either. Life as we know it is infinite. Don't get me wrong, Dan; we love life, but it's a different life than yours. I obsess that something may change for me in life. The difference between humans and my self is that I cannot experience time as you do. I was not part of your Big Bang. I have seen an infinite amount of Big Bangs like yours. Your type of life goes on forever, too, beyond many deaths. Your life is but a part of a bigger life sequence that never ends and in fact never began! In that way, your life is quite similar to mine. Remember that your Big Bang is but one of an infinite number of Big Bangs that have been going on forever, everywhere."

"What..." Dan began as he pondered his thought, "What could you possibly not like about living forever?"

"Well it's the same over and over for me, Dan. For you, there is some remarkable new life after death, a totally different life. I would like that. I have been able to trace your lives after death. I see that your chemicals, your new body compositions, come back to life again and again, ad infinitum. The universal life cycle never ends. It's your mind, your mental makeup that's a mystery, Daniel. When a human dies, I cannot see what actually happens to your so-called 'soul.' I can actually see it leaving your body but cannot see it after that. I believe that it lives on and can visit you in your dream state of mind."

"But what if that doesn't happen?" asked Dan. "What if it's all over?"

"Well, then, it seems that it is all over from your standpoint, Dan. What would it matter to you then, anyway? Infinite and being dead forever are the same. Humans cannot see out of the box to realize that."

"Well," Dan said, "If I'm just dead forever, then I know that I would have been cheated in life without having lived a good life. Maybe I wouldn't be as obsessive if I was leading the life that I was intended to have. I had the world on a string, and I was going to have a great life. I'm very upset why this has happened to me. I try to make the best of it. I use my poetry to try to be someone, to be successful at something, just like anyone else. What else can I do in my limited capacity? I was destined to be a successful lawyer. I was so much brighter than most people. I try to tell myself that I'm normal, but I know deep down inside that I'm not and that I'm not the same person that I used to be. It's like the real me had gone after everything changed. I remember who I once was, but I can't bring him back. It scares me and it hurts me, to have lost so much. But how can I go around saying that I'm not normal? That would be like giving up! I love my brother, but he doesn't realize the pain I'm in everyday. I can't show him."

"I see your point, Dan, but your brother knows more than you think."

TWENTY-NINE

It was twelve-thirty in the afternoon of the following day when we pulled into the town of Rigger, Virginia, off of the northwest border of West Virginia. It must have been named so for all of the rigs in the parking lot of this diner. After all, this was basically an exit off of the interstate highway. No sign of a town. For all intents and purposes, this was it, post office included. There maybe were about thirty houses within the town limits, but it was no town, just an extra-large truck stop.

After walking Oogie around the parking lot, Dan and I moseyed into the place.

"Hey, Dan, when was the last time you washed your armpits?"

"It's been a long time, Steve, a long time."

"I smell them. I guess we can get away with it here. Let's get a table so that you won't be too close to anyone."

I picked up the *USA Today*. It had been about three weeks since alien contact was made. Now it made front-page news everyday. This one stated that crime was on the rise due to contact. International tensions were developing. Murders, larcenies, petty crimes, acts of terrorism and domestic violence were spreading. This increase was due in large part to the riff between those contacted and those who had not been. I wondered why the entity would allow this to happen.

The non-contacted were doubtful of the contacted. Why didn't he speak to all? I didn't blame them for thinking like that. How could this be the right path to take? How much worse could it have been if the entity had spoken to everyone? Would there be more chaos than we'd already witnessed? Apparently there would be, according to the entity.

Another article in the newspaper written by a famous psychiatrist said that "so-called normal people" with borderline psyches tended to go over the edge at these times. They seemed to experience more difficulties than even emotionally challenged people for some reason. This was shown in the sudden increase in domestic violence, as well as roadside rage, both prime examples of such reactions. When upset, angered, or confused, these people found good enough cause to vent their frustrations by smacking their wives or children.

The food at this place was good yet nondescript. We ate and ran, in order to get back to our mission on the road. I knew that there would be many more diner stops along the way, and usually they got better the further south that we traveled.

We had been driving on the Interstate for nearly three hours when my brother moved up to the passenger seat up front next to me and a car passed us rather quickly on my left hand side. Without any warning, this car swerved in front of me as it tried to make the exit on my right. I slammed on the brakes and turned sharply toward my right to allow this person by. I hastily looked at Dan, then behind me at Oogie to see that he was all right. Everything was fine. Oogie had his ears up as if saying, *"What was that all about?"* I was saying other things myself, but in a different context when I thought that I heard my brother say something to me.

"What did you say, Dan?" But Dan was already up and moving to the coffee table seat in the middle of the van. Then I realized what was happening. I thought to myself, *it's you*!

"Yes," I heard, as clear as daylight.

I again thought to myself, *Is it all right to think instead of talk?*

"Yes, I don't mind," said the entity.

I nervously turned around to see if my brother was noticing anything, but he was involved in his own conversation, probably speaking to the entity as well.

"Are you speaking to my brother right now?" I asked out loud. Dan didn't notice.

"Yes, I am, plus a million other people. I hope you don't mind?"

"Not at all," I said, laughing. "It's not like you can't do that, I guess."

The entity didn't say anything.

"Hey, am I going to be all right driving?" I nervously asked.

"Well, if you can drive and think at the same time, I don't see why not, Steve. I want you to do one thing for me though, Steve," said the entity.

Yeah, what's that? I thought.

"I want you to remember that exit that you just passed with that car nearly hitting you."

Okay, I said to myself. *That was exit seventy-seven*, as I glanced up at the mile post marker on the side of the road. Just above the marker in a grassy knoll I saw a billboard that read, "THIS IS GOD'S COUNTRY, HAVE MERCY."

"So, where have you been?" I asked out loud.

"Oh, I've been around, I guess you can say," responded the entity.

"You know," I said, "sometimes I can't get in touch with you. What's up with that? I think that I'm going crazy at times, and I'm not sure if this is all real?"

"No, Steve, this is real," said the entity. "It is as real as that car that almost hit you. And that is what I am here to talk to you about, what is real, Steve."

"I don't get it," I said.

"Well, then, let me try to explain it to you," said the entity. "Real for you, Steven, is, right now, the present. The first lesson that you must learn is about time. To your astonishment, there is really no such thing as time. Even your Albert Einstein rationalized that fact one hundred years ago. He theorized that time was not a constant, that it can indeed change. Lo and behold, he was proven correct. Time does slow down the faster that you travel. Atomic clocks in your spacecrafts have proven that. So, doesn't it also make sense that time can stop?"

I couldn't answer.

"There is no time except right now in your mind, Steven. Do you think it's any different once you die?" asked the entity. "It's even more so once you die. And thank God for that, otherwise it would be a very long time for you to sit around waiting to be put back into another 'life-conscious' form, as you currently are. It would be never, if time really existed."

"So, Steven, time actually changes. That is when you realize that time, in fact, does not exist; when your lifetime is just a non-definitive part of infinity, a part of the whole living organism that we are all a part of, no beginning and no end, only the present, like right now—oh, Steve, be careful of this guy coming on your left!"

With that, I looked into my side view mirror to see a car go speeding by on my left- hand side and cut in front of me to make the exit ramp on my right-hand side. Dan was sitting in the passenger seat and yelled, "Watch out!" I hit my brakes hard as I swerved to my right. The speeding car went on its way to the exit ramp. I checked to see if everyone was all right.

Oogie was in the back, looking at me with his ears pointed up, and Dan was mumbling something as he moved to the back of the van again.

I looked ahead at the next milepost marker, which was number seventy-seven. Above it, on a grassy knoll a billboard read, “THIS IS GOD’S COUNTRY, HAVE MERCY.” I glanced down at my watch, which was the same exact time as when we passed this spot before.

THIRTY

The rest of the ride went by quickly for me. It was nearing six at night and I decided that we should head off the highway to find a place to stay. My brother and Oogie were both napping as I gazed their way. We had just entered West Virginia and were approaching a town called Canton. *Canton it would be for the night*, I thought, *if they have a motel.* This would be my official start of the Highway 21 flea market, since I knew that I wasn't far away. We exited the highway and turned onto Main Street. While searching for a motel, I came across a side street with an arrow pointing to Cacophony Lake. *Whoa*, I said to myself. *This would be a good place for Oogie to stretch his legs. How can I pass up a name such as this?*

Oogie had now moved up to the passenger seat, sensing that I had broken the monotony of steady highway driving. He was surveying the area as a potential pit stop. It turned out to be an interesting side street as we descended from pavement to gravel and then sand. Trees grew thick on both sides with overhanging branches rubbing against the windows. Oogie's interest piqued as he stood up in his seat and stuck his nose out of the window to get a better sniff of the surroundings. I made a decision to continue on, at least until the road got rougher.

A few houses came into view on my right-hand side. I slowed down as a courtesy but also to examine them more closely. They were run down and had miscellaneous items on the front lawns.

"We must be getting into the boonies," I said to Oogie. He looked at me intently as if he understood. People in the boonies always seemed to keep their belongings in their front yards. Maybe it was because they didn't have sheds in the back, or the backyards had already run out of room. There were bicycles, washing machines, old lawn mowers, swing sets growing rust, dressers, chairs, tools and bald tires. *Geez*, I thought, *this could be mistaken for the start of the flea market if these items didn't looked rooted to the ground.*

Something else caught my eye, which forced me to pull over for a better look. On the chain link fence surrounding the last house on the road were three squirrels sitting together silently, without stirring. The breeze was blowing the hair on their heads and tails back and forth as they stared directly at me. I got out of my van and slowly approached them. They didn't move. I stopped at five feet away to make sure that nobody was watching me and I got a much better view of these critters. I could now see that each one was skinned with a slit in their backs from their head to their feet. They were propped up with their heads positioned on the top of the fence. *Okay*, I thought, *I'd better step away easy and head back to my van*. We continued on down to the lake.

At the bottom of the hill, we entered a gully with another tattered sign pointing to the left for Cacophony Lake. We bounced along a potholed dirt road, which woke Dan up. Pine and oak trees appeared around us. Oogie began his cries of joy, knowing that this was a place that we would walk. He acted as if this was his first walk in the woods ever. I was steering right to left, avoiding monster ditches. I doubted my ability to continue on when the lake appeared on my left through the branches of the trees.

It was a pretty lake, perhaps one mile in radius.

"This looks like a good place to walk, hey, Oogie?"

Oogie showed his approval by jumping in his seat. We parked in a small clearing on the side of the road. Dan was now up and lighting a cigarette.

"Dan, we're going for a walk around this lake. Hang out. We'll be back in no more than a half an hour. Keep the doors locked if you want. It looks safe enough."

Oogie was out in a bolt. He ran into the woods seeking a stick. Not any ordinary stick, but a stick of high quality for throwing and retrieving, one that would meet the approval of the Kennel Club of America. He came back with a beauty, a piece of oak. Immediately, he dropped it at my feet for examination and for trimming of any outside bark and protrusions. He jumped at my side, awaiting my finished product. He always found a stick wherever we went.

We began our walk, crunching on fallen pinecones on a dusty curved road. Weaving through woods, we came to a clearing with Cacophony Lake on our left. I threw the oak stick sidearm, giving it a whirling effect, and Oogie jumped ahead to retrieve it. Nothing could be better in a Labrador's life. I stopped our trek, thinking I heard a car from behind me. I turned to look, but nothing was there. We continued on. Once again I heard the rev of an engine, along with the sounds of pine needles crunching. Each time that I stopped along the banks of the lake, there was no sound or vehicle approaching. I noticed that only when I walked next to the lake did I hear the sound; when we headed back into the woods, it stopped. We followed the road as it wound its way around the lake like a sleeping serpent, bringing us back to the van.

Dan was sitting inside, smoking another cigarette and drinking a diet cola.

"Well, we're ready to go find a place to stay and to eat."

"Good, I'm hungry," Dan said. "Where are we?"

"In a town called Canton, West Virginia. We did about two-hundred and fifty miles today. We're at this place called Cacophony Lake, Dan."

"Well, let's get out of here, Steve, it gives me the heebee-jeebees. Did you see those piney guys go by in their pickup truck?" he asked.

THIRTY-ONE

"We are all liable to the same errors, all alike the slaves of our respective dimensional prejudices."

Edwin Abbott, ***Flatland***

Heading along Main Street, I had the feeling of being in a make-believe town on a make-believe trip. Our primary concern was either a place to eat, or a motel, in whatever order.

"Dan, I don't know about you, but I was speaking to our friend this afternoon while you were sleeping in the back."

"Yeah, I know all about it," Dan replied.

"What do you mean you know?" I asked.

"I was talking to him also," said Dan, "and he told me about your conversation while I was dreaming."

"So, wait a minute, Dan. Are you telling me that you were eavesdropping on my conversation?"

"No, just that it was talking to me also, at the same time," he said. I laughed, knowing that it wasn't really important to me, but at the same time, I wondered if there could be no privacy with this thing. I heard no response.

Up ahead, a slight bend to the right of the road revealed a town. Tall elm trees on both sides of the road signified an entrance point. The town was small, with Victorian houses adorning its streets. Old- style lampposts, picket fences and long dirt-smoothed driveways were at every house. Not a neighbor stirred, not a car, a cat, a smell, nor wind… not a thing. It felt surreal. Dan and I were transfixed. We could sense it.

It seemed like a laid-back Sunday evening within a coma, and all were frozen in their rear dens.

At the end of this long Main Street of majestic homes was the downtown section of Canton, a once affable-looking business area with half of its stores vacated years ago. A medical office, newspaper building, lawyer's storefront, town office, haberdashery, drug store, and hardware store were the remnants of a past bustling town. The effect of the old- fashioned black-colored light posts was dramatic, augmenting a draconian feel to the Byzantine era. It gave Canton what appeared to be akin to a decent burial.

"Do you see anything, Dan?" I asked.

"Whoops, what's that?" Dan said, pointing.

On my brothers right-hand side was an old Coca-Cola sign hanging forgotten, crooked on one rusted chain, with a faded green base and orange color. I slowed the van down to a crawl as we both peered through the darkness and into what used to be a soda shop. A cold chill ran up the back of my neck as my mind resonated like an old tin can that had been kicked up the street into my senses, jolting me back to my younger days growing up in the Bronx. I could hear the sudden cawing of a lone crow, which gave me the eerie impression of it sitting with us in the back of the van. We both looked behind us. Meanwhile, the bottom section of this bygone, vintage sign read, "GOOD FOOD," as it creaked in a gentle breeze.

"What do you think, Dan?" I asked.

And without any hesitation he said, "Let's go check it out, Steve. It kind of reminds me of the old luncheonette that Aunt Mitzi had on Shakespeare Avenue in the Bronx, with Uncle Joe."

I freeze-framed to that place, where the juke-box played the doo-wop sounds and the teenagers did the Lindy Hop right on the checkered pattern linoleum floor. I could smell the cheeseburger and fries that Aunt Mitzi was cooking up for me as I spun on that nifty cushioned steel-plated stool at the counter.

I pulled the van in, parking headfirst. I told Oogie to wait a minute.

"Let's go see if it's open," I said.

We stepped out and stared at the front window of the eatery. Spelled out on the glass was the name "Eberneezer's."

"There seems to be a light on, Dan. Let's go in." I looked at my watch. It was just after seven. At the door was a sign showing the hours of operation.

"Well, it says that it's open until eight."

I could see through the pane glass window that the place was empty and dimly lit. I reached for the front doorknob, and to my surprise, it opened with the jingle of soft bells. We heard a lady's voice from the back of the restaurant call out that she would be there in a minute. The place had a cozy feel. It had a small counter of maybe five of those twirl-around stools that I used to love to spin on as a kid. There were about eight booths along the side and four tables in the middle of the room. It was a very old town place but there was a faint scent of incense burning.

Once again, the voice called out, telling us to have a seat wherever we'd like.

I said to Dan, "How about this one?" and we sat down. Outside of the restaurant on Main Street my van sat alone. Daylight slipped away into an envelope of darkness.

THIRTY-TWO

"How are you guys doing?" she asked. "My name's Lilly. I don't recognize you guys from around here."

Behind the counter stood an attractive lady perhaps in her fifties. She had natural blond hair that had faded with age to a whiter shade of pale. She was very pretty, with a nice figure from the waist up that was visible from our seats. I could not see below that point. She was wearing a black apron over her waist and had a cotton knit top on with the two top buttons undone. As she stood behind the counter and looked at us, I noticed her beautiful smile. I must admit that Dan and I were speechless. I was wondering if she had asked us anything.

"Oh, we're fine," I replied, hoping that was a sufficient answer for whatever she may have said.

She now stepped out from behind the counter and stood outside of its corner in full view of us. She was wearing snug-fitting Levi's jeans and they looked good on her. Her smile was mesmerizing, as my brother was non-verbal for the first time in years. She seemed legitimately happy to make our acquaintance. She was about five foot seven, slightly zaftig, but a nice zaftig! I admit that Dan and I were both taken back by her mere presence. Especially Dan, as it was not normal for him to be so quiet for so long. I could see that he was really checking her out and appeared to find her very much to his liking. Lilly seemed to be digging it.

"Lilly, this is Dan, and I'm Steve. We're brothers, and we're not from around here. We live in New Jersey, and we're on a diner and Antique Trails trip. We also thought that it would be a good time to get away from where we live with all this craziness going on. Actually, we live right next door to a nuclear power plant, and I was getting a little uneasy with all of this banter about terrorists and the threats that they pose."

"I see," said Lilly. "That sounds like a great trip you're on."

I looked at my brother. This was not like him. I was waiting for his usual conversation, which for some reason was not forthcoming. Usually he took over all interactions. I do believe that he was smitten. He stared at Lilly. This trip was now working out even better than I could have ever imagined.

Lilly had come over to the table while talking and asked if she could sit down with us while taking our orders. My brother surprisingly pulled out a chair next to him and motioned for her to sit. I could sense a chemistry that was brewing between the two of them. I was suddenly overwhelmed with happiness for Dan, as I smiled uncontrollably. *Wow*, I thought, *this could be interesting*. I hadn't seen this side of Dan since we were kids.

She adjusted her apron as she made herself comfortable in her seat. She looked at us both and then she spoke.

"Listen, guys," she said as she gazed at my brother, "I really can't show you a menu because I've been cleaning up inside for the night. We usually don't get much business at this time, but I can stir you up a hodgepodge of what I have left over if you don't mind?"

She then checked for our response. She looked at Dan first, but couldn't get a reaction from him, so I said that, "That would be a great idea."

"What do you think, Dan?"

In a voice far away, I heard Dan reply, "Okay."

My Jewish state of mind started to wonder, though,

how much might this cost? I was sitting there quietly while Dan and Lilly were involved in a little tête-à-tête, trying to control myself and just to let it slide. I was thinking about what my friends back at home would be telling me now: "Steve, let it go, just let it go! Live on the edge, big guy." Finally, overwhelmed by my wallet, I asked Lilly how much this was going to cost us. Lilly stared at me for what seemed like an eternity, as I could hear the clock on the wall ticking, ticking. While rising from her seat and with a pert smile on her pretty face, she said, "Don't worry about it, Steve, I'll take good care of you." Dan stared at me with indifference, while shaking his head in disbelief.

As Lilly stepped off into the kitchen, Dan and I followed her every move.

"Not bad," I said aloud. "Listen, Dan, I've got to go out and feed Oogie in the van. I forgot all about him. He's probably hungry."

I went outside. It was beginning to drizzle. After feeding the good old boy, I looked up through the windshield of the van to see Lilly and Dan engaged in a conversation at the table. I could see that she was smiling. As I came back in, the door jingled my return. The table had been set. Lilly asked me how Oogie was doing.

"He's fine, thanks," I said.

"I have a dog at home, too," Lilly stated. "Her name is Tobias. She's a great big old Saint Bernard. I love her to death! Listen, Steve, I hope you don't think this is too forward, but I wanted to ask you if you thought it would be all right if I joined you and Dan at the table for dinner?"

I immediately said, "Sure, that's fine," while looking at Dan as he smiled at me.

THIRTY-THREE

The smell of the food came wafting out from the kitchen.

I asked Dan, "What's going on here?"

He said, "I don't know, but she's nice."

Dan had the look of a cat that just swallowed a mouse.

Then she came back to the table with a large serving tray. She laid down a bowl of chicken potpie stew with a cinnamon-ginger crust topping which was bubbling all around its sides. She placed a dish of baked cranberry sauce and another rather large bowl of what she called cornbread salad.

"I hope that you guys don't mind, but this is what I was going to bring home tonight."

"Not at all," I said. "This smells great."

Dan said something about our Uncle Harry being one hundred years old and still smoking cigars every day, and I thought, "Oh, boy, here it comes!"

And it did.

The food was just incredible. And the conversation was funny as my brother became his usual self, and he filled the table with laughter and crazy insight. Lilly loved it. My brother took it into high gear and did his borscht-belt humor. He could do no wrong.

"So, tell as about yourself, Lilly," I said.

"Well, I don't know where to start," she said.

"How about this name for the place, Eberneezer's?"

"Well, Eberneezer was my dad, and he owned this place. Moved here and bought it in the fifties. He died about ten years ago. I took it over about fifteen years ago when he was no longer able to run it. Canton has never been a big town, but it has always been big enough to support us. My mom, Tillie White, passed away when I was a young girl. I don't even remember her. I was always very close to my dad. I was an only child."

Dan asked Lilly how old she was now, and before I could tell him that that was not a proper thing to ask, Lilly said, "Fifty-seven years old."

"Fifty-seven," I said. "You look great, Lilly. Wait a minute. You said that your name was Lilly White?"

"No, I didn't say that. But you figured that one out, Steve. Nice going. That's right, I'm bright and right, I'm Lilly White!"

"Wow," I said, as I stood up to excuse myself from the table. "I'm sorry to break away from our conversation, but I have to walk Oogie since I fed him just before."

"Oh, that's fine," Lilly said. "You can take him through the alleyway and into my backyard behind the restaurant."

On that note, my brother got up to make one of his daily pit stops. Lilly also stood up, saying that she had a pot of decaffeinated coffee brewing, along with some sweet potato raisin pecan pie in the oven.

As I was standing in the dark looking through the back screen door, I could see Lilly getting the dessert ready. She was singing as she went about. She was actually happy that we met her. Who was this lady that we bumped into tonight? Looking at her and just being in her presence gave me a feeling of being with my long-ago-deceased sister, Carole. My eyes were beginning to well up as I thought of my sister taken away too early from this life. She was older than Dan and me. She would have been sixty-seven years old now. It had been over forty years since her death, yet this lady Lilly evoked images and feelings akin to my sister for some reason. She was always there to protect her two younger brothers. And many a boy got their hides kicked by her because of that!

Back inside Eberneezer's, we had some incredible pie and coffee. When I gazed upon the clock on the wall, it was nine-fifteen. I interrupted my brother from one of his no punch-line jokes to say that we should get going.

Lilly looked at me with puppy-dog eyes and asked, "Where are you guys going to stay tonight?"

"Well, I was going to ask if you knew of a motel in the area, Lilly," I replied.

"Oh, we don't have a motel in town and the nearest one would be about twenty miles up on Route 21. Listen," Lilly said, "I know that this sounds forward, but it's not meant to be. But you guys can stay over at my place for the night, if you'd like."

Dan and I looked at each other and gestured with our heads nodding up and down like two of those bobbing baseball heads that you sometimes see in the back windows of cars in New York City.

"I've got to bring my writing along with me," Dan said.

"That's awful nice of you, Lilly," I responded. "Are you sure that we wouldn't be putting you out too much?"

"No, not at all. And I wouldn't have asked in the first place if I thought otherwise."

"I have to bring my poetry, Lilly," Dan said.

"I'd be happy to read it, Dan," Lilly replied. "I've been waiting for you to offer some of it to me. Just let me close up in the back, and I'll be out in a minute."

I could see my brother's eyes light up like a child

who had been accustomed to so much despair and torture over the years.

"What about the dogs, Lilly?" I asked.

"Oh, I think they'll get along fine. My Tobias is a big lover, she's a girl, and your Oogie sounds like a mush boy," I heard her say from the kitchen.

"Yep, that he is, just like his daddy," I said. "Listen Lilly, how much do we owe you?"

"Oh, that's all right. It's on me," she said.

When Lilly reappeared with her denim jacket on that made her look even younger than she was, I handed her a twenty-dollar bill. She stared back at me funny and said, "What are you doing, Steve? I don't want that."

"Lilly, please take it. Dan and I want to share with you. We are grateful for your friendliness and for making us feel like family."

"Okay," she said.

I could see that she was touched by that and took the twenty reluctantly.

"I'll pull my car around to the front, and you can follow me home. It's only yonder down the road a bit."

THIRTY-FOUR

Dan and I were in the van waiting for Lilly when I asked Dan how far a yonder is.

While driving through downtown Canton, I realized that we were the only two cars on the avenue. It was dead silent, as if the sleepy town had been tucked into bed for the night. We came to a blinker light with an intersection on the right. There was a gas station closed up for the night and a small church on the opposite corner. We turned on to Leechville Road. Houses became sparse amid farming fields, and then woods. About two miles later, Lilly put on her right turn signal. We pulled into a driveway similar to the ones that we passed in downtown Canton, dirt-filled sand and stone, compacted over time. We bumped and rambled our way past her house toward the backyard. We could hear Tobias happily barking at her master's arrival. Oogie was up and yapping in reply.

The house was one of those that I always wanted. It was cabin-style with a triangular roofline running down its sides, adorned by second-floor dormers. It had a look right out of one of those supermarket magazines touting the best country-styled homes to live in.

"Dan, this is nice," I said.

Dan replied, "I feel more like I'm at home now, Steve, than I have in years."

I looked at Dan, slightly perplexed. I also felt something strangely familiar, emotionally. I couldn't place it, but I sensed it, too. We parked the van and came inside. As I opened the back door, her dog bolted outside with Oogie in pursuit. Lilly asked us to hang up our coats in the closet.

“I see that Oogie and Tobias are hitting it off in the backyard,” mentioned Lilly. “Can I get you anything?” she asked.

“No, we’re all right, Lilly,” I said.

“Well, make yourself comfortable. I’m going upstairs to change. The dogs will be okay in the back. There are no cars around, plus I have a doggy door on my back door, so they can go and come as they please.”

Dan and I sat down on an old soft colonial couch. It showed its age with its sunken seat cushions. *How many years of tales have been spun here?* I thought. I could sense the warmth and coziness of this living area. There was a stone fireplace withered with soot and a stack of oak ready for more gatherings. Older colonial furniture, paintings in antique frames, pine wood beams running the ceiling led to the shoe-worn landing of the stairway rising to the second floor.

Oogie and Tobias came barging through the doggie door that appeared to be the size of a barn. They already seemed to be best of buddies as Tobias was following Oogie around.

“Good boy, Oogie. Seems to be you got yourself a girlfriend, old boy,” I said. I reached out to pet Tobias, who was a beautiful old Saint Bernard of orange, white and dark colors. Tobias sniffed at my leg and sensed that I was Oogie’s friend. She sat down to let me pet her as drool hung out of her jowls. When I stopped, she immediately lifted my hand back up to her head by flipping it with her nose.

“Well done,” I said. From across the room, sitting in a tethered armchair, Dan exclaimed, “I think that I like this girl.”

“Oh, it’s only your imagination, Dan,” I responded in jest.

"What do you mean by that, Steve?" Dan objected.

"I'm just busting you, Dan. I couldn't help it. I think that she really likes you, too. You may have hit the jackpot, old boy."

"I've got to have a smokie," Dan said, as he reached into his pockets for a crumpled soft pack of non-filtered cigarettes.

"Maybe you should go out to the back to smoke," I suggested, thinking strictly out of courtesy.

"But she's got an ashtray filled with butts right here," Dan declared.

"Yeah, you're right, Dan," I apologized. "It's your choice."

Dan lit one up.

"I've got to go to the bathroom, Steve," Dan remarked.

"Well," I said, "there's one off of the kitchen in the back there, where we came in."

Dan got up to go, leaving the cigarette burning in the ashtray. I thought to myself, *Two smokers, I'm in for it!*

Lilly came downstairs. She had her hair untied now, and it even made her look five years younger, hanging shoulder length. She had put on a bulky sweatshirt over comfortable pajama-style pants. On her feet were those furry soft slippers in the shape of two puppies. She sat on the couch next to the chair where my brother was sitting.

"I see that Dan found my ashtray," she said.

"Yeah, he thought you wouldn't mind," I said.

"No, not at all. Make yourselves at home."

Oogie and Tobias lay next to each other, lost lovers found. Dan came back from the bathroom with his hands still wet from not drying them thoroughly, a common habit of his. He delightedly took a seat next to Lilly. My heart skipped a beat as I watched Lilly take a doily off of the armrest of the couch to dry my brother's hands with. My mouth gaped open as I felt tears well up from this caring gesture. Most unexpectedly, Dan picked up what was left of that cigarette, which was now a burning butt, and placed it between his nicotine-stained fingers for that final bit of inhalation satisfaction.

"Listen, guys," Lilly said, "there's something I've been meaning to tell you, but I didn't feel right until we got to my place."

Oh, boy, I thought. *I hope this isn't the part where she gets up to shoot us now!*

"I remember that you were talking about all the craziness back at the restaurant. And since we were hitting it off so nicely back there, I really wanted to get you guys over here to talk with you about it. In these parts, most people don't accept this voice contact. I really can't tell many folks that I have contact with her or they would think that I've gone crazy. So you see, I don't usually get a chance to speak to anyone about it. Down here, folks tend to be very religious and not very open-minded. I have a business to run, so I'm better off keeping my mouth shut. If they ask me if I've heard any voices, I just shake my head no and say, 'Oh, my God, no!' If anyone else has had contact, I'm sure that they're not going to admit it, either. I have one friend in town, and she also has spoken to her."

I blurted out, "You called it 'her'."

"Yes, she," Lilly responded.

"Well, it's he and she to me," Dan said.

I was miffed. I didn't know that Dan spoke to both.

"Steve, it incorporates whatever gender you would

prefer listening to, or perhaps expect to hear," Lilly said. "And you know this for a fact, Lilly?" I asked. "Funny how I got a man," I said, dejectedly.

"Yes, it was one of the first conversations we had. We talk almost every night," said Lilly.

"Get out of here," I said. "I don't get to speak that often."

"Listen, guys, after I feed Tobias, I'd love to have all of us make contact tonight. What do you think?"

"Sounds great, Lilly, but I thought that he only speaks to everyone individually," I said.

"No, that's not the case at all. You've got to open up a little, Steve, be more like your brother over here."

"Come on Steve, don't be so anal" Dan joined in.

"I'll show you guys. I promise you, it will be enlightening," said Lilly.

THIRTY-FIVE

"In my father's house are many mansions"

King James Version, John 14:2

With a cup of hot chocolate in hand and a crackling fireplace, we sat cozily on the two-piece colonial couch. I had not realized how chilly it could get in the foothills of West Virginia for this time of year. Then again, I could not be certain if this was a normal temperature for this time of year, or if this had something to do with our visitor affecting the weather. Dan was sitting next to Lilly, quite content, while I was by myself on the loveseat section.

Lilly said, "Okay, here we go."

She sat with her eyes closed, holding on to my brother's hand. I could make out her mouth moving ever so slightly, as if she was muttering under her breath. I myself was enraptured, leaning forward, feeling my blood pulsating. Then, from behind me, I heard his voice, its, or whatever it was, speak. It was the same familiar voice to me.

It was a gentle voice. He was a person, a thing at ease with himself. There was emotion, humor and all of the human qualities associated with speech. But his was eloquent and soothing. As if for the very first time, I examined his speech. I found it appealing. His voice was similar to a late-night disc jockey's on a cool breeze jazz station that could put you to sleep.

"Hello, Steve, Dan, and Lilly."

"Hi," we all said in unison, although my response came out muddled.

Lilly mentioned that the voice she was now hearing was that of the woman's.

"How is that possible?" I asked. "I hear him in the male's voice."

"Easy," it said. "Whatever voice that you want to hear, you will. There is more that is possible than your logic alone implies, Steve. There are things that you are not aware of or would be able to comprehend."

In mid-sentence his voice changed from the familiar one that I was accustomed to, to that of a female's with the same tone and pitch.

"Okay, that's okay," I heard myself mumbling.

"So, how is it going?" it asked all of us.

"Fine," Lilly replied. "Dan and Steve want to know why you speak to me everyday and not to them?"

"Well, that is due to my experiences. As I have said prior, I pick and choose the times and places. I do this with you in mind, according to your way of saying what is relative to the circumstances. Is that not so, Steve?" asked the entity.

I didn't know what to say. I felt as if I was back in school and the teacher had just asked me a question I couldn't remember the answer to.

Haphazardly I said, "Yes, everything is relative. Everything must be judged by its own criteria. Although things may look identical, they will never be exact."

"Very, very good, Steve. Where did you ever pick up that logic from?" the entity asked.

"I don't know," I said. "I've just come to reason that over time."

"Well, it happens to be universally true. Not many understand that, Steve."

Lilly gently applauded while my brother looked on with a wry smile.

Oh, boy, I thought to myself. *I must be tripping.*

The entity continued, "As I was saying, I do this with you in mind. I realize how fragile this visit is. Most of my visits are precarious. Everything that I do has to be planned with the well-being of each world in mind. When I speak with Lilly everyday, it's beneficial to all parties involved. If I am aware it might be otherwise, I would not do it. That is why I do not speak at times or to certain people. Everything that I do and every way that I act is calculated to cause the least amount of disruption. If I did not do that, there would be far more chaos than you see."

"So tell me," I asked, "was your visit here planned?"

"No, Steve, I have never planned a visit. My visits are incidental. My thoughts and my actions are planned, all within my present state of being. I am free-willed to move about, but am all-encompassing and all-seeing, wherever I am."

"Wow," I said, "that was heavy."

"So," Lilly asked, "you have not come here to save our planet or for any reason in particular?"

"That is correct," responded the entity. "I see that your planet can use some help, but my presence is purely coincidental. I do offer my wisdom."

"Well, could you tell us what is going to happen to us in the future?" asked Lilly once more.

"I am sorry, but I can not do that. For some reason beyond my own understanding I am not able to. Yet I see things beyond your existence here and beyond the fate of this planet.

Then Dan spoke, "You are God, aren't you? After all this time, I've really been speaking with God!"

"No, Dan, I am not God. If I am, I don't even know it. I question my own existence, yet I do believe in God."

"No, I still believe that you're God," said Dan. "If you are not God, then who are you and where are you from?

"I come from nowhere, the same as you," replied the entity.

"No, I come from God," replied Dan. "We come from our mothers, through God's Will.

"So do I," responded the entity. "Although I have no mother, I, too, come from God. But believe me, I am not God. How we differ is in the understanding of the concept, Dan."

We sat, trying to absorb what we were hearing.

"Now, before we end our talk for the night, I want to leave you on a much lighter note. We have someone else who would like to participate in our conversations. Actually, there are two of them."

"What are you talking about?" Lilly asked, as she abruptly stood up from her seat next to Dan's.

I was bewildered once again. My brother was taking this the best of all. Lilly was looking around the room and outside of the windows for two other people.

"All right, all right, take it easy," the entity said. "I will let you speak to them. Please, sit."

Lilly sat down again next to Dan. For the first time since meeting us, she was exhibiting a different side to her personality. She now seemed apprehensive, just as everyone does at times. In fact, we all became apprehensive, awaiting our new visitors. Lilly, though, seemed more so than us. Perhaps she believed it would be her loved ones that had passed. I also thought they would be mine.

Oogie and Tobias entered the room as if sensing a commotion.

"Here, boy," I called to Oogie, for him to sit next to me.

Instead, Oogie and Tobias stopped in a position facing both couches and then sat parallel to each other, able to view the three of us. Oogie and Tobias were sitting in the same position that I had observed Oogie in when he was in a trance on our hike in the mountains. Then, Oogie tilted his head to his right and stared at me. Tobias did the same with Lilly. That is when they both started talking to us.

THIRTY-SIX

I awoke on the living room couch. I picked up my watch lying on the coffee table. It was seven. It was one of those wake-ups where you are disoriented, unsure of where you are. I thought I was home on my sofa until I opened my eyes. I first gazed at the ceiling and found it strikingly different. That's when I jumped up to stare at the room, confused. Then it all sank in. I must have fallen asleep here last night, and Lilly had thrown this blanket over me.

Wow, I thought, *what a dream I had. I dreamt that the two dogs were talking to us*. Man, it almost seemed real! Now it was all coming back to me. We actually had a three-way conversation with the entity. I swore we must have spoken to the dogs. All that I remembered was that we started laughing hysterically. They actually had voices. How was that done? As soon as I heard Oogie's voice, I must have passed out from laughing so hard.

Their command of language was very limited, too. I remember mostly words, no sentences, such as "hey," "good," "love", "stay," "boy," "girl," "walk", "eat," "yum," "out" and "go." Still, I sensed that I understood him last night. I looked around the room to see where he was but did not see him or Tobias. I got up, went to the bathroom, then walked through the kitchen to the back door. Looking out in the fields. I saw Oogie and Tobias playing. She was about twice the size of Oogie, but was rolling on the ground submissively in front of him. They were happy. *This is a great place to live*, I thought. *It's a beautiful house with privacy, a great piece of property and in the country.* The sun was up, but a chill was in the air that you could actually smell. It had the aroma of a bouquet of wild flowers, with a hint of hay and grass.

On my way back through the kitchen, I passed the downstairs bedroom and peeked in, since the door was ajar. I could make out a huge comforter with what appeared to be two people under it. I thought to myself that Dan must have gone to bed with Lilly last night. *Good for Dan! It's been quite a long hiatus for the guy, seven or ten years and perhaps thirty-five years since he last had a meaningful relationship. He deserves it.* On the kitchen table I saw a note.

It was from Lilly. "Hi, guys. I hope you slept well. I had to open for breakfast. Please make yourself at home. You know that you're welcome to stay if you want to. If you'd like, you should come into town for breakfast or lunch. Whatever the case, I want to say that meeting you has been special. It seems as if we're family, and I don't even know you! And Dan, you are special. I want you to know that I meant everything I said last night. You have my number, and I have yours, so please call. I will call if I don't hear from you. If you decide to continue on your fantastic adventure, which I wish I was a part of, then you must turn right outside of my driveway and continue down five miles until you come to Route 21. You'll see signs to go south on route 21. Steve, take care of Dan. I'll see you again. Luv, Lilly."

I felt happy for my brother and thought I would ask if he wanted to stay with her while I continued on alone. That could wait til he got up, since Dan was a late sleeper and I didn't want to wake him now. Still, I was going to try getting him up at around ten if we wanted to get going today.

The dogs came through the doggie door. They went

right to the bowl of water and gurgled and slurped joyfully. Oogie followed Tobias into the living room to lie down next to her, both trailing globs of drool along their way.

I made myself a pot of coffee, turned on the kitchen TV, and sat down at the table. It was now seven-thirty as I flipped on the morning news. "WXYZ, the Morning Show. I'm Stan Dorsey, along with Sue Lockman. Here are the top stories of the day. The oldest nuclear power plant in the country was attacked last night. The F.T. McCormach Power Plant in Griffen Bay, New Jersey was attacked last night by terrorists. The attack was thwarted by state police, National Guard and The Air Guard reserves. Three terrorists were apprehended while another two were killed. It happened last evening at approximately seven-thirty, when three terrorists slipped into the northern gates of the plant driving a late model sedan. They pretended to go over to the visitors' center, which was already closed for the day. Once on the plant property, they veered off the visitors' road and headed toward the actual plant. They had a mobile missile launcher, which they managed to fire one missile from. The missile missed its intended target and landed in the brush, starting a fire in the adjacent woods. Meanwhile, state police and other security officials surrounded the vehicle and apprehended the three terrorists."

"While these three were placed into custody, the second phase of the attack began. A light model twin prop airplane was then used to attack the plant by launching three other missiles, which did manage to hit the plant. One hit the cooling tower, while the other two hit the reactor building. Power Plant

Officials maintain that damage was superficial. A Black Hawk helicopter was summoned and destroyed the plane. Two bodies were later recovered from the wreckage.. No other fatalities or injuries were sustained on the plant premises. The plant has been closed down temporarily and has been placed off-line until further damages can be assessed. Plant officials have said that there have been no radiation leaks. All five terrorists were described as being of varying descent. One suspect was quoted to have said, 'This attack was in direct retaliation for American and Israeli propaganda regarding phony claims of alien contacts. These claims are used only to incite unrest and chaos among Arab nations. It is a deceitful plan being used against our people.' And we will be back after this short break."

I stood up to get a cup of coffee. My head was spinning, as this was the power plant next to my town. I couldn't believe that my reason for leaving came true. Thank God that catastrophe was averted. I sat down with my coffee and poured in some milk and sweetener. The news came back on the air.

"In other news, more attacks of violence have sprung up in the Middle East regarding the alien contacts. Israel has warned Palestine, Syria, and Iran about future attacks and the shipments of weapons. General President Ian Clancy of The United World Nations has asked for a ceasefire to all violence in the area.

Turning to news regarding the alien contact, scientists have now confirmed actual contacts. Tests have been performed verifying authenticity. This is not a hoax according to Secretary of Defense Doctor Norman Lewis. Doctor Lewis has asked of the entity to provide further proof for nonbelievers. He believes that the entity cannot be seen and is invisible. The entity has not spoken to everyone on Earth, therefore leaving some to doubt. We ask that the world remain calm, as this entity does not pose a threat to us.

In a related topic, The National Weather Service has now confirmed that this last year has set a record for the most abnormal weather behavior in our nation's history. Record rainfall and snowfalls have been set for the current year. We have had the most tornados and droughts on record. Experts believe that this is due to global warming and not the alien.

On a much lighter note, the Yankees have lost their ninth straight game last night, rekindling rumors about the firing of their manager."

I poured myself a second cup of coffee. It was eight o'clock. I looked into the bedroom and saw that Dan was still sleeping. There was no need to wake him now.

I decided to take the dogs for a walk into the woods behind the house. It was an unbelievable feeling to have nobody around for miles as we hiked through a forest of twenty- foot pines and thicket. Upon returning to the house, I decided to call my buddy Charlie back at home.

"Hey, Charlie, it's me, Steve. Can you hear me all right? Yeah, listen, I'm out in West Virginia, some town called Canton, I think?"

"So, did you hear about the power plant up here, Steve?" Charlie asked.

"Yeah," I said, "I just saw it on the news this morning."

"Those crazy sons of b's, Steve, they went ahead and they finally did it. I never thought it would happen here."

"Well, thank God there was no radiation leak, Charlie!"

"Yeah, that's what they say, Steve. But how can you believe anyone these days? Did you know that they made us evacuate the area?"

"No," I said, "they didn't mention that on the news."

"Yeah, they did. We just got back this morning. We had to get a motel room forty miles inland. It's been a real pain in the butt, ouch! I had to move Mom and Uncle Carl. You should have seen the traffic mess. They're still out there for hours, fighting with each other. This evacuation plan they have is just a bunch of crap. Maybe thirty years ago it could've worked. Now there's way too much traffic for the roads to handle. The sirens went off, and most people did not know it was an evacuation. It took the police hours going through the streets with loudspeakers and knocking on doors to get people out. The smart ones stayed. I think that most people just stayed."

"I'm sorry to hear that," I said. "Dan and I took off for our road trip earlier in the week. We'll be gone for four or five more days."

"Can you believe the havoc this thing is causing?" Charlie asked.

"Yeah, I'm not surprised that people freak out when you throw them something new," I said. "What about you Charlie? Do you believe in the entity?"

"Oh, yeah, I do now. At first, I never spoke to it, but since it contacted me, I know that this thing is real. It's freaky, Steve. The world has finally been contacted, and like wild animals, we act insane."

"Well, Charlie, maybe we are insane?"

"I never thought that it would happen this way, Steve. Whatever happened to the flying saucers and the spaceships?"

"I don't know, Charlie. It's funny how things never

work out the way that we plan. Listen, buddy, I've got to go. I hope there are no leaks. I'll see you later."

"All right, Steve, I'll see you when you get back up here. Maybe we'll go for some Chinese, if there's still Chinese."

THIRTY-SEVEN

"Grand Cardinal Sephus, I am here to speak to you. Can you hear me?"

"Yes, I can hear you. Can others also hear us talking?" asked the Cardinal.

"No, Father, only you. You do not have to speak out loud for us to talk. I can hear your thoughts, and you will mine."

"And what should I address you as, my friend?"

"Friend' is fine. Father, I thought that it would be most appropriate to speak to you here in your house of worship, the Basilica of the Blessed Saints. Is this all right?"

"Yes, fine, I would prefer it, so that my Lord will be present, too. Let me ask you, my friend, did you hear my prayers that I desired to contact you?"

"Yes, Father."

"My friend, who are you? And why do you speak with me when it has been said that you do not prefer to speak with heads of state, or religious leaders?"

"Father, I will answer the later question first. I have spoken with some heads of state and some men of the cloth. I chose to speak with those of an open mind. You are open-minded, Father. I find that a high quality in you, since you are also devoted to our Lord at the same time."

"Yes, I am. I guess that it's kind of a hypocrisy, my friend, that I can be both."

"No, Father, I don't think so."

"I consider myself an ordinary man, an inquisitive man. As a man of reason, I ask the same questions as my fellow man. I do not believe that it is a sin to wonder, to probe, and to inquire," explained the Cardinal.

"That is why I am here, Father."

"Well, you have still not answered my first question, my friend."

"Yes, Father, I am an alien from another place. I am your first alien contact. I may not be what you expected to see or imagined I'd be."

"Well, let me be rather blunt, my friend. Are you the Devil?"

"No, Father, I am not. How can I make you believe otherwise?"

"I don't know, my friend. But that is what a lot of my congregants and comrades are saying about you."

"Father, all that I can say is that you must trust your own heart, Pray to God and see that I have done no harm."

THIRTY-EIGHT

"So, Dan, what's the story?" I asked.

"With what?" Dan responded, as he took a drag of his generic brand of smoke. I could always tell when Dan was dragging on a generic. He had a foul look upon his face, a scowl, a look of partial disgust, as if to say, "This is not a Camel."

"What's the story with you and Lilly?" I asked. No reply, as Dan was apt to getting into one of these moods now and then.

"You know," I said, "you could have stayed with Lilly. I asked you back at the house. It would have been fine with me. I would have picked you up on the rebound if you wanted. Or you can just flat out stay with her. That's all right with me, too. I'll take you back if you want to go," I propositioned. *Too many questions*, I thought to myself. *Now I'm sounding like a Jewish mother, kvetching.*

Dan took another drag on his cigarette.

"When are we stopping for coffee?" he asked.

"As soon as we get to the next diner," I replied. "Dan, do you like her?"

There was no reply. Dan wasn't talking. For some reason, he would get this way from time to time. I didn't know if it was one of those times, or if it was over leaving Lilly. This was part of his makeup. It was Dan. I had learned to put up with it, just as he had learned to put up with me. Dan stood up from the front passenger seat and carefully found his way to the coffee table behind me. Apparently, he couldn't take any more of my prying.

Many times Dan would say, "You can't read my mind." He would always want to make sure of that. I certainly couldn't. I wished he knew that. I heard him mumble that once again, as he reached his seat.

Dan started to cough. It was not so much a smoker's cough but more of an acid reflux symptom. He had this condition for many years now, built up from smoking, poor eating habits, and the cocktail of medications administered for his ailments. In the past, I would take Dan into the hospital for a day procedure to scrape his esophagus clean in order to allow the flow of food and fluids. It had become more difficult to convince him to go on each occasion. He hadn't been in for quite a long time now and was willing to suffer its consequences. His coughs had now increased to a rapid succession, as he couldn't stop.

At times, this would go on for hours while Dan refused any assistance. "Just leave me be," he would struggle to tell me. He would often lie down and wait hours for the episode to pass, since the coughing was followed by severe heartburn. I feared for his health, thinking that he would damage his lungs or heart from the severe hacking. I became tolerant though, instead, and soon learned to back away.

Oogie took over in the copilot's chair. I turned to look at him and noticed that he was staring at me intently once again. I started to laugh. *Oh, oh*, I thought, *he's probably attempting to speak to me again and wondering why I'm ignoring him today? Oh, boy, I've got a lot of explaining to do to him now.* The more that I laughed, the more upset he became. He was giving me that short, pert bark, "Arrff!"

"I'll bet you have something good to tell me," I said. "Oh, yeah, after last night's intelligent conversation, you're wondering why I'm not jabbering with you again." *Yep, he's probably telling me that I should have left him behind with his girlfriend Tobias.* I was getting mistreated by everyone today.

"She's a nice girl," I heard Dan say from behind me.

"Yeah," I said. "She really likes you, Dan. I think she wanted you to stay."

"I know she did," said Dan.

"Well, why didn't you? I wouldn't have minded."

"No, Steve, this is our vacation, and there's a lot more diners out there to be tested."

I laughed again. "You've got that right, Dan, you've got that right," I said. Just then, I caught Oogie's stare once more. He hadn't taken his eyes off me since the last time that I looked. That meant only one of two things; either he had to go to the bathroom, or else he was hungry. Now I realized what Oogie was telling me. I hadn't fed him this morning.

"All right, Oogie, I'll feed you in a little while, as soon as we stop for breakfast or lunch." It was nearing two.

THIRTY-NINE

"Father, may I ask you what is wrong with your world and why does religion seems to be at the crux of the situation?" asked the entity.

"My friend, I was going to ask you the same."

"Father, I have seen this before in many worlds such as yours. But I have also seen many such worlds at peace. The problem here is that many persuasions are fighting over the same God. But each persuasion claims a true God, while all others are labeled false. I have seen worlds of the same religion. I have seen others of multiple faiths, yet neither fight over beliefs."

"Yes," concurred, Father Sephus. "There seems to be a great hypocrisy here. We have killed each other throughout our history, the Crusades, especially."

"Yes, I have read your different Bibles with the same stories but with different names. It all seems to be one and the same to me," replied the entity.

"And you, my friend, what do you believe in?"

"Father, I, too, believe in a supreme maker. Whether I call him God, He, She, or It, what difference does it make? None, Father. It's as if your world has the right concept but goes about it shearing heads in the process. Very disturbing, Father. This attitude is seen in people beyond religion. It is epidemic in world politics and then filtered downward into simple human relationships. You tend to forget that your world is one living organism, a whole of many parts. That whole cannot be healthy if its parts are sick."

"I, too, my friend, believe as you do. But I cannot stray too far from my faith. I see the hypocrisies that you see, but I have been taught by the Bible and centuries of teachings to maintain my belief."

"But Father, you have the power to try to change that hypocrisy. Your world is at odds because there is never sufficient proof of your beliefs. So instead of proof or rationalization, you then call for a steadfast blind faith. You say that you must 'just' accept the Written Word. This is where you go wrong, by excluding differences. Why not bridge evolution with creation? When it's one or the other, heads start falling off. Don't you see the conundrum, Father?"

"Yes, I do, but I am in a position of leadership that has been passed on for centuries in a prescribed manner. You are asking me to shatter tradition?"

"Yes, Father, I am. Who else can but leaders such as yourself? You can make a difference! Please, Father, let me go on. There are times where blind faith and rationalization both fail. Eventually, they both always will. The question regarding one's belief in God is a prime example and exactly what we are talking about. It is the age-old paradox of what came first, the chicken or the egg? If God made life, then where did He come from? You see, Father, there is no need to run away from this question and to bury one's head in the sand, much like an ostrich. This is a time to accept the unexplainable, along with one's faith."

FORTY

"Dan, Charlie called me this morning to tell me that the power plant was attacked last night."

I didn't know if Dan was listening, but I repeated the whole story. Dan was still moody. He lit up another cigarette. I was hoping it was a Camel. Soon after, we entered a thirty-five mile speed zone, a sure sign of a town. We stopped at the intersection of Route 21 in Calvin, West Virginia. This was designated as the official start of the Antique Trail.

"Can we get something to eat?" Dan suggested.

"Are you feeling any better?" I asked.

"Yeah," was all that he replied, as he took in a deep inhale of his Camel.

We had lunch at John's Diner. I fed Oogie in the van while Dan went inside with his poetry notebook and pens. The town was alive with vendors, shoppers, tourists and regular town folks. It was the first day of the festival. They had vendors set up with their tables on the sidewalks, as well as the empty parking lots. It was a brilliant summer day, one that you wanted to stow away in your back pocket.

I grabbed the local *Georges County Gazette* and sat down to have lunch. Dan was busy showing our waitress, Bonnie his writing. Bonnie was being as polite as could be yet appeared relieved to see me coming.

"Hi, Bonnie," I said after noticing her name tag.

"Hi," she said back. "You must be Danish's brother Steve?"

"Yes, I am," I replied. " Dan, did you order yet?"

"Yeah, Steve, I'm getting some zoupie and tea to play it safe. I gave Bonnie my order. You were right about the power plant, huh, Steve?" Dan whispered.

"Yeah, Dan, I guess so. It was just a hunch I had, a bad feeling, I guess. Thank God that nothing happened. That had the potential of becoming a major nightmare."

"I'm going out to have a ciggie," said Dan, as he stood up gingerly, trying to gain his balance.

Finally buoyant, Dan did his routine of picking up his pants by the sides and pulling them upwards many times to make sure they were steadfast. He was now ready to shuffle in his Charlie Chaplin style. And shuffle he did, as he stopped only at various booths occupied by customers to do his famous, patented Danish two-step. This was where he would make enough noise from shuffling to announce his presence. Sometimes Dan would improvise a smoker's cough if that did not get their attention. Once Dan had them captivated, he would then come to a complete halt in front of their table, only to do that backward, forward motion, kind of like the back and front steps of the cha-cha. As deftly as Muhammad Ali, floating like a butterfly, annoying as a bee, my only hope was that no one would grab him, wondering what in the heck he was doing. To my surprise, nobody did. Usually, he would get a smile, or shake of the head. Dan only wanted to be accepted as a regular guy.

After an hour and a half of seven smokes and five coffees, our waitress was happy to see us go. Yes, Dan and I were going to torture every waitress at every diner along the way. No coffee cup was to be left undrunk. Although, we gave at least twenty percent on every tip, unless, of course the waitress was from hell, and then we'd make them work for it. Bonnie was legitimately ecstatic as we exited.

"Dan," I asked, "do you want to check out some of the antiques with me?"

"I can't walk much, Steve. But I'll go a little ways with you. Did I take everything out of the diner with me?" he asked.

"Yeah, I think you did, Dan. Do you have your smokes and glasses?"

"Yeah, I think so."

"Well, why don't you check now before we leave, to be certain?" I asked.

"Yeah, I have them, Steve. Did I take my meds today, Steve? I don't remember."

"That I don't know, Dan."

Just then my cell phone rang. It was Lilly, of all people. I gave the phone to Dan and then unlocked the doors, opened the windows, and left him to check out the antiques.

During my stroll, I spotted a *USA Today* in its newsstand. The headlines read, "Emergency Summit Meeting Called for Today at The United World of Nations." Yet I couldn't concentrate on the story. Instead, I was thinking of my brother, realizing that over time he had been losing his ability to walk distances, even short ones.

FORTY-ONE

The meeting began at three this Monday afternoon. All nations were present via video conferencing. Scientists, military, political leaders, presidents and prime ministers of all different nationalities were present. The corporate conference center of the United World of Nations was hosting the meeting. The UWN President Ian Clancy led the proceedings as its spokesperson. The United States delegation consisted of Doctor Norman Lewis, Secretary of Defense; Vivian Neary, Secretary of State; Doctor Ivan Chekaras of the NOMAD Command Center in Nu Daz, New Mexico; Press Secretary Scott Knolls; and President James Smith.

"So what do you think, Scottie? Do you think this thing is going to talk to me?"

"Well, Mister President, it said that any and all could attend."

"'I guess I'm going to finally hear this thing?"

"I think that you---hold on a second, Mister President. I think that the meeting is starting."

"Ladies and gentlemen, can you hear me and see me as well? I am General Assembly President Ian Clancy of the United World of Nations. I have been asked to host this meeting. It is a pleasure to accept this invitation, having such historical significance! As you are well aware, many leaders of the world have been requesting such a meeting in order to quell the many questions and doubts that we have in regard to our visitor. Hopefully, this meeting will alleviate the tensions that we now face. The entity has agreed to attend this meeting, as it has become an issue of necessity. Upon its arrival to our planet, the entity did not want to cause panic. Based on its own experience, it decided to wait to speak to everyone. Today, though, ladies and gentlemen, we stand together on the threshold of greatness for mankind! The time has come for perhaps civilization's greatest moment. For today, we will speak as a planet to our first alien contact. I know that many of you attending this video broadcast have already spoken with the entity one on one. Some of us have not. For the latter, it is our first time. Hopefully in the near future, you will be able to speak to our visitor on a personal level. The entity has maintained that is your preference. But it will not speak to anyone that does not wish to be contacted. We will only be able to hear our visitor, since it is invisible.

"Therefore, ladies and gentlemen, without further ado, let me introduce you to our guest. For those in our auditorium, I ask that you put on your headsets that are sitting next to you. The entity has advised us that it would be preferable to hear its actual voice with the use of our headsets. There will be no translation through the means of our facility, as the entity has promised to do that for each and every one of us. It would rather you hear its actual voice but cannot do that in our auditorium without the use of the headsets. I suppose that some of you maybe wondering why it cannot speak to us telepathically? We are doing this so that each headset can be recorded for authenticity purposes, according to the entity's permission. Additionally, the voice of the entity will only be heard as a males voice today, also for verification purposes. Ladies and gentlemen, hold on one second, please, one second please..."

For what seemed like an eternity, a great pause was

observed. All present waited in anticipation. Some could not move, dumbfounded, while others leaned forward in anxiety, rocking back and forth. The world awaited an historical event. The headsets crackled for a few seconds, and then the entity's voice came softly into the ears of everyone in the room and watching on TV.

"Good afternoon, ladies and gentlemen!" You could hear the audience respond with excitement as they turned to speak to their friends sitting next to them. A few seconds passed until the chatter subsided. "Or should I say, greetings, Earthlings?" At this remark the audience exploded with laughter and cheering.

"I thought that might lighten up the moment for us. But isn't that what visitors to your planet always say?"

Once again, the room filled with laughter and clapping.

"This is truly a great moment for us. Although I have visited countless planets, each encounter is as great as the last one. I know that there has been great confusion as well as overwhelming concern in regards to my arrival and actual existence. Right now, many believe my voice to be a hoax. It is very hard to prove to each one of you my authenticity. Above all else, though, you must believe that my visit is one of friendship and good intentions. Why I have only spoken to a select few up until now is intentional on my part. My experience has led me to believe that this is the best method for you. May I address you in your customary manner as ladies and gentlemen?"

Much of the audience responded yes. Still others sat with their mouths wide open.

"I know that you have many questions, and believe me, I will answer all of them. If not here, I will answer them in private with you later. Here, we want to answer one question at a time for authenticity's sake. Everything will be recorded today.

"Who am I? The number one question. I have no name. You may call me those words that you have chosen, the entity, it, friend, et cetera. I have come to your planet only by chance. I know that you may find that hard to believe. I am a nomad. My home is my identity. I move throughout what you call space, and the mind. Although we are vastly different, I will try to explain myself as best as I can. Remember, I will have ample time to speak to each of you before I leave your world."

No one spoke anymore, caught up in the entity's story.

"You are wondering why I am invisible? It is because I am not from your dimensions. I do not even exist in your time dimension, for I know of no time. It is different for you and me. I am here now speaking with you, but for me, this thing that you call the present is the same, all of the time! I do not have a future or a past. I was never born, and I suppose that I will never die. These are human qualities, which are exclusive only to your universe, and the infinite others like yours. You experience this thing that you call time because of your epic beginning, which began for you at the moment of your so- called big bang."

The audience in the UWN began to whisper to each other, awed at how the entity didn't need anyone to speak to know what everyone wanted to know.

"What do I look like? If you could see me, I would resemble a gaseous cloud with no shape or dimension. But my lack of shape is only according to your mind and logic. My size can be any. It can be infinite, or it can even be nonexistent, invisible to you. Where have I heard that expression… that size does not matter? I can't place it, can you?"

It only took a matter of seconds for the audience to erupt into a crescendo of laughter, as the entity demonstrated what would be called excellent stage presence as it waited for that right moment to continue.

"I know that is a hard concept to digest, but it is the truth. It goes beyond your method of reasoning, but stay with me. There is much more to what is out there than meets your eye! You can only see three dimensions with your invisible time as a fourth. There are more dimensions in your own universe that are hidden from you, visibly and mentally. I am from many other dimensions, both inside and outside of yours. The numbers are infinite. Yet I can traverse your universe and make myself known to you and others. It seems that my purpose in what you term life is to encounter all consciousness and to enlighten all. What will come as a bigger shock to you is that there is also life within your dream state and beyond what you call death. You are vain as a civilization but can be excused for such shortsightedness due to your infant state of being. Therefore, I exist not only in your visionary awakened state but also in your dream state and mind."

All present were hushed, like a Sunday school class of children being admonished.

"I mentioned before that I know of no such thing called time. For myself, there was no beginning, and there will be no end. I have existed forever. For you, though, you live and die in this time element. Let me be clear, your intuition and senses are still a vast area, unexplored. For you speak about the soul and the hereafter, but have no proof of its existence. But if you live long enough as a civilization, you will come to know, although you may never prove it outright, that they do exist! You will come to know that your mind is the portal to these places. And your mind is actually a hidden part of what your eyes see, and cannot see in the heavens above."

The audience shifted in their seats, eager to hear more.

"Oh, yes, one other revelation before moving onto some questions from the floor. Are you alone? Far from it! There are many like you. There are even more that are different from you. The numbers are infinite. I hope that doesn't ruin your day"

FORTY-TWO

"Let's go, Dan. I didn't see anything that I liked."

"What are you looking for, Steve?"

"I'm looking for paintings from famous artists."

"Yeah, right, and you think that people are so dumb that they're going to sell you that?"

"Well, yeah," I said.

"Well, then, you're more delirious than I am, Steve."

"I think that you might have a valid point there, Dan."

We drove through the edge of town. Dan lit up another generic cigarette from behind me.

"When you see another store, could you stop for more smokes, brother?" Dan asked.

"Yeah, sure," I said. Dan didn't reply.

"I thought that you had plenty of cigs with you?" I asked.

"Yeah, I do, but I want to get some Camels. I can't taste these," Dan said. And that's how it went. The smoke was driving me crazy. I smoked up till a couple of years ago. It wasn't the urge to smoke one that was driving me nuts, but all of the smoke that was hanging in the van. Even with a couple of windows open, it was of little help. I had promised myself that I would put up with the smoke, since we both wanted to do this type of trip for years.

As I said before, people with emotional illness, depression, and the like are more prone to be smoking addicts than the general population. It seems to be one of their insatiable cravings.

Up ahead on the highway was the first of many flea markets set up along the side of the road. This one was a huge one with a parking lot behind the tables in an adjacent field. It also had a couple of main buildings, including a gas station and a Brown Cow convenience store.

"Well, I think that you'll get your Camels in there, Dan."

It was very crowded out there, and Dan took a look and asked me to get him three packs of Camels. With his equilibrium messed up and his fear of imbalance, I went for him. I could never tell if this was a part of his anxiety, the medicines that he took or something physical, but I was noticing it more often lately. After dropping the Camels off, I proceeded to walk around the flea market with Oogie in tow.

FORTY-THREE

"The floor recognizes the first question from the gentleman from London, England."

"My friend, my name is Daniel Palmer from the Royal Division of Ministries. In light of your comments regarding the increased capacities of our dream state as well as our minds, I would like to know if you, in fact, can dream as well as us?"

"Mister Palmer, I find it amusing that I cannot dream. That is a faculty of only certain living beings, especially the kind from your dimensions. Yet I can see the dreams of others. Isn't that strange? I can also see departing souls upon one's death. I see them leave the body, but I do not know where they go. They reappear again in your dreams, quite amazingly, where I see them again. I have determined that they are, in fact, the same energy source that has left the body, except now they still can communicate with you through your dreams."

"Did you know, Mr. Palmer, that certain animals, such as your dogs, can actually sense the departure of the soul? I see that this is a revelation to you, but your scientists will soon be able to prove this matter, within reasonable doubt, of course. It's just a matter of time in your world. Funny how dogs cannot see colors like humans, yet they can sense the soul and have the ability to smell a hundred times better than humans. All conscious forms of energy have different abilities. You cannot see me, yet I have clear images of all of your dreams. I believe that I cannot dream because I am a part of the actual dream state," the entity continued.

"May I ask, Mister Palmer, do you doubt that you have a soul?" asked the entity.

"Well, I'm not sure, Sir Entity. I believe that I do

from my religious upbringing, but I believe that it is quite normal for me to doubt this as a person."

"Ahhhh, very good Mister Palmer, an honest man! Never assume anything. I don't. And neither would God, except for the goodness in your heart. Thank you, Mister Palmer. May I have the next question, please?"

A brief moment of silence followed until the General Assembly President spoke again.

"The next question will be from the President of The United States, President James Smith."

"Mister Entity, it is certainly an honor to finally speak with you. Let me ask you, Mister Entity, if there is anything that we can do to help the current state of world affairs that we are experiencing?"

"The pleasure is mine, Mister President. Above all, everyone should remain open-minded. That would create less derision. The first thing that you can do is to stop the destruction of your planet. I have seen it done before. Your situation has been played out many times, and it forecasts gloom. It is brought on by greed. Your greed has woven itself into your basic institutions. It starts at home. How each person treats others is felt throughout the world. Your world is rapidly being destroyed, and you have trouble acknowledging it! It could be too late."

"What can we do to save it, Mister Entity?"

"Mister President, that is up to you. I have described to you your problem as clearly and succinctly as possible. The rest is up to you. Don't expect me to clean up for you. You have a world that has evolved with division. You are not as one. You are not whole. You may be independent, and that is not bad, but you must be as one. I have discussed this issue with your politicians and philosophers. I am a prime example of being one and many. Of course, we are different life forms, but all life that flourishes is one with itself. You are selfishly depleting your resources and you act as if you don't care. Nature always wins and continues on."

Everyone silently tried to absorb what the entity was saying.

"Due to this dilemma, hatred festers. Too many are starving and dying of hunger and disease, while still others hoard riches that they could never use in their lifetime. Just stop right now. Think of what I just said. Don't let it pass on by as if it didn't mean anything. What are you going to do about it, nothing? Are you going to propose a commission, or pass it off to your Congress and the legislators that your people elected to make decisions? Well, then, good luck, because they will be fighting over politics instead and won't make a decision even in the time that it takes me to leave and come back in a trillion years."

"Can you help us?" asked the President.

"You ask me to help, President Smith? What do you think that God would do? There is too much hypocrisy here."

There was stone cold, dead silence in the audience, as well as in all of the broadcasting rooms throughout the world, as the President sat back down on weakened knees.

"Thank you for asking the most important question of all, Mister President," said the entity.

"The next question is from the Physics Institute of Japan, Professor Yamato Yukihiro."

"Our visiting friend, we would like a bit more clarity about the whole picture of life that you have described."

"Professor, I will try. First, and above all, you must all come to terms with the fact that anything is possible! Outside of your box, which is your universe, there is infinity. I know that you are not sure about that concept, but there is a lot that we are all unsure of. I can only be 99.99 percent sure of it myself, simply because infinity never ends. I have told you that there is no record of my beginning. How could there be in infinity! Imagine this, for this is what I actually know through my travels. You and I are one looking up into the heavens as far as we can see. We are like the cells in a body. Outside of this body is another body that we live in, much like our own. This other body is peering up into another sky, also looking into another universe much like your own and is thinking the same thing as us! He is also enclosed in another body and so forth and so on. This succession of events is actually going on as we speak. I have traveled there as well and there is no end to it."

"Another analogy that I can offer would be your Mandelbrot Principle. This is the principle that states that all life in nature repeats itself in successive generations. You see this when looking at the rings of a tree as well as in human generations passed on. There is always a great similarity in each generation, one that is almost mimicked, in fact, thus allowing for a mirror effect. This effect was discovered by a man named Benoit Mandelbrot through the aid of the first computer microscope that he invented at IBM. Astonishingly, this effect was also seen in inanimate objects as well, such as a slice of a rock, or the satellite image of a coastline as when viewed from above. Therefore, magnifying an image, or relying on the computer to simulate beyond its scope, all leads to one conclusion. Whether we look microscopically, or macroscopically, all things repeat themselves within their life process."

At this point in the discussion, the audience began speaking with their neighbors in disbelief.

"Why are you all acting surprised? Apparently, many of you are not aware of this man, of this great discovery! You must become more knowledgeable and therefore more open-minded! I hope that this is a sufficient answer to your question, professor," the entity replied.

"As for myself, I am not a part of this life cycle. I am merely a part of infinity."

FORTY-FOUR

We were lucky to find a parking spot very close to the flea market tables and stores. Dan pulled out a lawn chair and made himself comfortable while enjoying one of his Camels. He was already engaging himself in conversations with any and all who strayed too near. I left him in his glory as he took a mighty deep inhale of satisfaction. Most innocent folks passing by were magnetically drawn to his cadence. There was something about Dan that was magical regarding how most strangers loved meeting him. Many, many years ago, centuries past, people of my brother's state of mind were burned, hung, or tortured by many, including the Church. Nowadays, thank God and thank religion, people were more tolerant and understanding of the emotionally challenged. They could tell right away that something was wrong with him, but they loved talking to the man. At first it was an act of kindness on their parts to stop and reply to Dan. But once he started talking, they were held in disbelief. He was far out, and he didn't hide it. They found him refreshingly different, intelligent and unique from the usual meaningless chitchat.

"Hi, how are you?"

"Okay."

"What's new?"

"Nothing."

"Okay, see ya."

"Yeah, see ya..."

They laughed at his poetic jive and jokes with no punch lines.

I didn't have that ability to be so congenial with strangers or anyone, except for the occasional "Hi!"

I took Oogie out to the field behind the parking lot for his walk with his stick. When we came back to the van, Dan was still holding a wife and husband captive. He was on what appeared to be his third Camel.

"Hey, Steve, could you get me a diet soda out of the van?"

"Yeah, sure, Dan."

I put Oogie back inside of the van and opened the windows to give him more air, as it was getting hot outside.

"Dan, I'm going to take a look around. Keep an eye on Oogie," I said.

I had my trusty Art Price indicator book to help me identify unknown paintings. I hid this book in my back pocket, out of sight. I did not want anyone to think that I was on to something. If I, in fact, came across a prospective painting, I would walk away nonchalantly, acting as if I had not seen anything of interest. My heart would pound as I tried to remember the artist's name while scurrying to a hiding place to see if he or she was in the book. If I found something noteworthy, I would then return and circle the painting, trying to ascertain if it was a print or an original. Eventually, I would return to the item and inspect it up close. I still had troubles discerning prints from originals. A real Detective Clouseau, I was. All the while, vendors were doing their best to keep from bursting into laughter.

These vendors were very crafty. Some of them looked like they were art dealers, which led you to believe that you were being taken. Other vendors would look as if they just came out of the woods, intentionally wearing raggedly torn clothing, with an insane look on their face, and then you knew that you were being taken. And if you had a normal-looking person, well, then forget about it, because you were definitely being taken. I could size them all up. Yes, I could. They were not going to fool me. They were *all* out to get me.

Right at about that time I found myself staring at a Renoir, old, beaten up and forgotten. My heart skipped a beat, and I started to sweat profusely through my baseball cap. *I wondered if the vendor had noticed me? Did she see me staring too much? No, she appears to be looking the other way. Okay, I have to make myself look as if I'm not in the least bit interested in this painting. Here, let me stand up from my crouching examination and pretend to show interest in the other crap she has lying around.* I slowly made my way out of her sight and immediately looked at my art-price indicator book.

"Oh, boy, here it is, Auguste Renoir, eighteen forty-one until nineteen nineteen." I casually sauntered back to the painting. *Good, she's not looking at me. Could it be an original of his? Oh, crap, there's no initial or first name on the canvas. Geez, I can't tell if this is a print.* The sweat poured out of my head through my cap and onto the floor. I was losing whatever composure I thought I had.

Okay, let me size this vendor up? She's dressed like a dirty mountain person, so she's probably poor. She has this older fellow sitting in a lawn chair behind the counter, looking like her dad. He, too, appears poor, as if he's a nursing home castaway on a daytrip outside of the facility. So far, so good! Let me mosey around a bit and listen in on their conversation. Oh, crap, here she comes!

"Can I help you, sir?" she asked, ever so friendly.

I decided to remain calm and do my Jackie Gleason

imitation of Ralph Cramden of "The Honeymooners."

"It's awful hot out here today" I said, as my sweat poured out onto the ground. I swiped at my brow. Then I stuttered as I tried to get the words out of my mouth. "No, no, no, noo noo, not really," I managed to respond.

I figured that might throw her off for while.

"You know, on second thought, maybe you could help me," I said. "I was wondering how difficult it is to become a collector-vendor such as yourself?"

This fine-looking lady of African descent, perhaps in her fifties, stood back as if to examine me more closely.

"Well," she said, "It's a lot of work. I'm a full time professor at Mid-County Community College down here, and my dad is a retired art dealer. And yourself?" she politely asked.

"You," I heard myself mutter. "Oh me, I'm a nothing. I mean, I'm retired and just travel around."

"Oh, I see. How nice. Are you interested in that painting over there that you were looking at?"

"Oh no, just looking, you know?"

Oh, boy, I thought, *she's on to me. And she probably teaches art at the college as well. I've got to get out of here quickly*, I thought. *I'm suddenly not feeling that well.*

"Ahh, what painting was that? I asked.

"This one," she said, as she led me back to the Renoir.

"Oh, this one, haha. Wasn't he a famous artist?" I laughed and at the same time sounded astute.

Once again, this fine lady in sheep's clothing stood back to analyze me with what appeared to be a slight snicker on her face.

"Yes, he was," she said. "He was Auguste Renoir."

"Oh, I see," I responded. "That's a nice print."

"I'll sell it to you for forty dollars," she bargained.

"Oh, no, thanks, I was only looking, thank you," I said, as I started to back away rather quickly. As I broke into a trot, I could hear her say, "Thirty dollars, we're closing up."

FORTY-FIVE

The members of the United World of Nations were held spellbound. Finally, Spokesperson Clancy introduced the next question. “Your Entity, our next question comes from Bishop Joseph Matumbo of Liberia.”

“Our friend, it is by the remarkable grace of God Almighty that we have been given this opportunity of enlightenment with you. Our heavenly friend, may I ask if you believe in the Heavenly Father and His Son, Jesus Christ?”

“Bishop, what if I were to say that I had never heard of a Jesus Christ? Would that make my belief in God any different than yours?”

“Yes, I believe that it would, your Entity. For it has been written down in the Good Book that you must believe in God and His Son for redemption and for deliverance into heaven.”

“Bishop, I wonder how that is possible? I, too, have faith in God. Because I am not privy to Jesus Christ, does that make my faith in a Maker more or less pious than yours? That does not sound reasonable, Bishop.”

“Reason and logic are not the answers, your Entity. In order to be saved, you must be baptized into the Lord and His Son.”

“Bishop Matumbo, I have not come to you and asked you to change your belief in God. How would you like if I asked of you to worship in a different way, or else be damned? Why should anyone’s belief in God, regardless of gender or affiliation, make any difference?”

“Because that is the way of Our Lord, what our Good Book says. You seem to need logic to believe, your Entity.”

"Bishop, God would want His children to use logic and not to follow blindly. Logic tells me that only a God could have made this world."

General Assembly President Ian Clancy quickly broke in to the discussion.

"Ladies and gentlemen, let us please move forward here, thank you. We do have one more important issue that we should address. Our Council members have asked for one special request of the entity. Due to the violence and acts of terrorism witnessed recently in response to your arrival, we are asking for a special sign, so that these disbelievers may end their heinous acts. These people refuse to take part in our discussions with you. They believe that your visit is a farce, purposely arranged on our part as a devious plot."

"We believe that a massive act of terrorism is in short order. Is there some way that you can show all of the world proof of your existence?"

"I have tried to talk with every inhabitant of your world,' President Clancy. "It is impossible, though, if they are resistant to my efforts. Others believe that I am the devil or evil. I will accept your request, Secretary General Clancy. Although I will show a sign, disbelievers may never accept this truth. In short time though, I will provide proof beyond my voice."

"In exchange for my assistance, I ask of only one stipulation on your part. I want you to remember what I have said about time today. It is most relevant to your needs. I want you to examine how you spend your time here on your planet. Think of the now and the present. Do good things out of the kindness of your hearts now and not later. And if you do this, my sign will then also come in the form of time."

FORTY-SIX

"Come on Dan, we ought to get going," I said, while still on the run.

"What's up, Steve, what's the rush?" replied my brother.

"Oh, nothing, I didn't see anything that I liked. It's four-thirty. We should maybe hit a few more flea markets before we start looking for a motel," I suggested.

"I've got to take another leaky, Steve," Dan informed me.

"All right, why don't you use the empty laundry detergent container in the van, Dan?"

"Well, it's full, Steve.

"You should have told me that. Look, the public bathrooms are over by the entrance. I'll drive us over there and you can use them."

Dan and I went into the men's room. I was emptying Dan's portable urinal in the toilet when he asked me about the woman who was staring at me in the flea market.

"Oh, that lady," I said. "Whew, I had to literally run away from her, Dan."

"I didn't see you run away from her," Dan replied.

"Wait a minute, Dan. How could you have seen that lady from the van? I was way over on the other side of the lot talking with that vendor lady."

"Vendor lady, what vendor lady?" Dan exclaimed.

"Okay," I said, "let's get this straight. Did you follow me over there and see me?"

"No, I was right here sitting in the van. She was a young lady, maybe in her thirties with dark hair and sunglasses on," Dan said.

"Okay, now you've got me going," I said. "I didn't see anyone following me and how do you know that she was staring at me?"

"Well, when you left me here, she was walking behind you and then stopped whenever you stopped. She made believe that she was looking at something else, every time."

"Come on, Dan, you have to be kidding me."

"Yeah, Steve, I'm kidding you! I'm always wrong! Why don't you believe me once in awhile?"

"I believe you, Dan, really. Every time that I doubt you, I always find out that you're telling the truth. I'm sorry that I sound that way. Why was she starring at me?" I asked.

"How do I know, Steve? Do I look like Mandrake the Magician? I need a cup of coffee, Hitler!"

I could tell that my brother was upset. He would get like that if someone doubted him or asked him too many questions. It made it difficult to carry on a long conversation with Dan when he felt that way. He would often say, "You don't know what I'm thinking," thus protecting the final vestige of his dignity. "You can't take that away from me. Nobody knows what I'm thinking."

"Why don't we stop somewhere and just sit for awhile?" Dan asked me.

"Nah, I don't think so, Dan. We got to get going. Anyway, it's too close to dinnertime. But I will stop and get you a coffee to go at this Brown Cow here."

We stopped at two more flea markets along the way. I did buy one interesting painting that appeared to be an original. I also had Dan join me for a short walk and he bought an old poetry book and a wristwatch for five dollars. It was nice having him by my side, as his physical well-being prevented him from venturing too far. It reminded me, though, of times past when he would lead me down the streets of New York, a different time, a distant era.

We pulled into the town of Hibishaa, West Virginia, around six-thirty that evening. We got a room at the Nightie-Nite Motel for thirty-five dollars. I wouldn't make up such a name. When we inquired about a place to eat, the desk clerk, an older skinny guy named Earl, told us to try Andy's Diner a bit down the road.

Dan could only eat some scrambled eggs since he was still having some difficulty swallowing. I felt guilty eating southern fried chicken with sweet potatoes. The food was surprisingly good for a small, non-descript diner. Even better was that they had a television on, and we got to see the evening news with their local affiliate news anchor Barbara Lindsey, from channel two Charleston.

Dan was outside having his fifth Camel when the news began. The lead-off story was about the entity's meeting today with prominent world leaders. It was an earth-shattering event, as the people of the world were able to hear the alien speak for the very first time. Many questions were asked. There was a heated debate between Bishop Matumbo of Liberia and the alien. At issue was one's belief in God, along with the acceptance of Jesus Christ, as the only path to salvation. General Secretary Ian Clancy asked the alien to show the world other proof of its existence beyond its voice contact. This proof was needed in order to ward off a possible terrorist attack posed by disbelievers, which could happen in the very near future. The entity reassured the world that by tomorrow, Tuesday, it would have its proof. In return, though, the entity asked the world to heed its prior reminder that time was of the essence. Dan came back in.

"Yeah," Dan said, "that girl was following you all day long."

"You mean the lady who was staring at me?" I asked.

He shook his head, "Uh-huh."

"What do you mean that she was following me all day?"

"Well, she was staring at you earlier in town after we had lunch. Then I saw her later in the day following you at the flea market. She has long, dark, curly hair," he said.

FORTY-SEVEN

"Now, can I tell you something?"

"Yes, sure, Mister President."

"This is all very hard to believe. Being a devout Christian, I would think that I'm going out of my mind or having a dream," said the President.

"Well, Mister President, apparently you have come to terms with yourself by accepting this," said the entity.

"I have. It's unbelievable, talking with you today and tonight. I've got to make sure that the little lady doesn't hear any of this, you know? I don't think that she's quite yet ready for this, being she's more devout than I am."

"Okay, Jim, I'll give you a heads-up if she's coming," said the entity.

"Listen, tell me a bit more about how we can straighten out this mess that the world is in," said Jim.

"As I was saying this afternoon, Jim, it doesn't matter much what I say if the world won't act upon it. My primary concern is to convey a message of dire need that your planet is in peril."

"Okay, friend, what can we do about it?"

"Well, Jim, it's a two-way street out there. I've talked about the bloodshed throughout the earth's history. Life here seems to be about survival of the fittest. Humans try to control everything, from nature to their selves. When you start messing with nature, though, you're in a losing game. Your destruction of nature, along with your narrow-mindedness of religion, is to blame."

"But my friend, you still haven't told me what to do."

"Jim, I have. I'm not going to write a script for you. I can show you better than tell you."

"How's that?" Jim asked.

"Remember when I spoke earlier today about the Mandelbrot Microscope, Jim?"

"Yes, I do."

"Well, I can use that same concept for showing you how others see you."

"My God, entity, what are you talking about?"

"Come with me, Jim, over to your closet mirror."

"This is not going to hurt me, is it?" asked the President.

"No, Jim, I'm not here to hurt anyone. Are you prepared to see yourself as other people do?"

"Yeah, I guess so?"

"Is that a question or an answer, Jim? Because we don't have to do this."

"Yes, I am ready to see what I appear as."

"Fine. We will use your closet mirror as the microscope. I will use my mental state of being to act as the fractal computer. I will use you as the subject in the mirror, Jim. Now all that you have to do is just watch."

President Smith looked at himself in the mirror. Nothing appeared out of the ordinary. Then for a few seconds, he thought he saw himself moving, although he was not. He could see his fingers twitching ever so slightly in the mirror. But he wasn't moving them! He felt strange, as if watching himself on television.

"Oh wow, I don't know if this is cool," he told the entity.

"I'm here with you, Jim. I want you to know that the same principle of the fractal microscope is in effect. Just as the microscope can look deeper into an object, so does my bend of your mirror. Just as the fractal shows the rings of life in a tree, so does my mirror show your past. I am able to do this Jim, since time doesn't exist for me. I am letting you view what I can see through my concept of time. All of your actions appear as one, forever."

The President was now watching many of his important decisions played out in speeches, world economics, as well as the battlefield. He felt as if he was dreaming, viewing himself as a bystander, similar to that of an out-of-body experience that people feel when they get close to death.

"How are you doing, Jim?" the entity asked.

The President did not answer. He was tripped out. He was seeing the good things that his country had done as well as the questionable things. He was feeling anxiety and anguish, all at the same time. He uttered at one point, "Oh, we didn't do that." The rings of events were shedding, like those of the tree, inside of the mirror. But the mirror reflected much like a stone thrown in a pond of water, ripples of circles moving out from the center. His past was being peeled, much like the layers of skin on an onion.

"Jim, you did do that. You are just seeing things from a different perspective, the other side. Now you see and feel what the other side feels. Can't you see the disharmony in your world? I have shown you the fighting over dwindling resources, the control over economics, the stealing of lands, and the genocide of innocent humans. Do you see how your inaction and questionable deeds have caused the call for retaliation? Don't get me wrong, Jim, your country has performed many good deeds, but it is always the bad ones that get remembered!"

"Thirteen percent of the world, eight-hundred and fifty-two million people, are starving every day. That is one out of ten people. It isn't that your world hasn't enough food but that the world is lacking necessary methods to distribute it. There is enough food produced in your world each day to provide four pounds per person. What in God's name is your world doing with it all?"

Every word the entity said made the President sob uncontrollably.

FORTY-EIGHT

After dinner Dan and I drove through town and passed by a small coffee house on Main Street called the Town Square. We checked back into the Nightie-Nite Motel and freshened up for the evening. I took the opportunity to feed and walk Oogie. Later, at around nine-thirty, we drove down to the coffeehouse to see what kind of action was going on in Hibishaa, West Virginia on a Monday night. We left Oogie in the van, where he always preferred to be, rather than in a strange motel room waiting to see if I would ever return to get him.

It was dark and dingy as we set foot inside the coffee house. Our eyes adjusted, and we could make out dimly lit glass candles on about ten old weathered pine tables on a cracked wooden floor. Only two of these candles were lit, however. There were only three other people inside the establishment, sitting at one table in front near a makeshift stage. A soft voice called out for us to "Have a seat," and "Make yourselves comfortable, fellows."

We walked over to the counter area on our left hand side to speak to the man who had called out to us.

"How's it going, fellows?" he said.

"Not bad," said my brother in reply.

"What can I get you guys?"

"Can we get a couple of decafs?" I asked.

"Sure. Grab a seat anywhere you'd like," he said, as he turned to get our coffees.

The counter area had ten bar stools, unoccupied. Dan said that he was going out to grab a smoke.

"Hey, you can smoke in here," said the guy from behind the counter. "You know, in most places down here, you're still allowed to smoke inside."

Dan turned around with a big smile on his face.

"My name's Tony," said the man from behind the counter.

"I'm Steve."

"I'm Danish, or Danishaa," said my brother.

Tony responded, "Well, that's a different name, Danish. I suppose that I've heard every name, but I've never heard that one. Did you ever have anyone try to eat you?" Tony asked as he laughed out loud rather heartily. "Like with a coffee, haha?"

Dan failed to see the humor in this as he responded, "I'm Dunish Tunish, the greatest poet ever!"

"Well, then, it's a doggone honor to meet you, Dunish," replied Tony in a down-to-earth fashion.

Oh, boy, I thought. *My brother is off and running. He's found another victim.*

"You know, Dunish, we have poetry recitals here. So later on if you're up to it, you're more than welcome to jump up there on stage and to wing us some of your stuff. Here're your decafs, guys. Oh, by the way, my friends call me Biggie, because as you can see, I'm of wide girth. Basically, though, I've just been eating myself to death! But, you can call me Tony, Biggie, Bigs, Mister Biggs, or Big Boy. Whatever you want to, fellows. Just don't call me a fat bastard, hahaha! Welcome to my place." As Tony turned to wipe the counter, my brother asked me for my cell phone.

"Who you going to call, Dan?"

'I was going to call Lilly."

"All right, do you have her number?" I asked.

"Yeah, right here in my wallet. Would you dial it for me, Steve? I'm not too good with these cell phones," he said.

"Sure, Dunishaa," I said. "Better yet, I'll enter it into

my memory for your future use."

I gave Dan the phone after entering her number and then dialing it for him.

"I'm going out to have a smoke and to speak to her," Dan said.

Tony drew out a Marlboro of his own and asked me if I minded.

"No, go right ahead," I said.

"Want one?" he asked.

"No, thanks, Tony," I said. "I gave it up awhile back."

"So, let me ask you, what's up with Danish or Dunish?" Tony asked.

"Well, Tony," I said. "Danish is my brother, and his real name is Dan. Dan is what you would call emotionally challenged. He was not like that all of his life. He had a very high IQ and was in law school when he decided to hitchhike to California in the late '60s. He was an honor student up until then and was a role model to me. Something happened to him, Tony, which the doctors could never pin down, and he returned back home a completely different person. He became who he is now, half the person he was mentally, physically, as well as emotionally."

"Ah, hell, I'm sorry to hear that, guy," said Tony wholeheartedly. "You know, Steve, I have a lot of friends like that. How old's your brother?"

"He's sixty-one," I said.

"I thought so. He's my age. And you take care of him, don't you?" Tony asked.

"Yeah, Tony, I watch out for the guy."

"You're a good brother, man! I could tell it when you guys started talking, and I could hear the care in your voice and see it in your eyes," Tony said.

"No, Tony," I said. "He's a better brother than me. He would have always done more for me. With what he's been through, I could never do enough for him."

"I knew it," Tony said. "I had you pegged for that answer. Never take the credit, man. Right, Steve?"

In came Dan with three new friends at his side. Dan was doing his little two-step jig as he walked. I knew then that I was in for an eventful night.

"Pardon me, Steve. Let me get these people seated. You know, tonight should get a bit crowded in here with all that Antique Trail stuff going on. And we got a singer in here tonight, a real crooner."

With that, Tony walked, or to be more accurate, waddled away, from behind the counter. He greeted the three new customers and led them to a table near the stage. I was astonished to see that Tony was, in fact, maybe five foot-two inches tall and was almost as wide as he was tall. But through all of my shallowness, I could still see that this man had a big, big heart.

"Hey, Dan," I said. "What's up?"

"Shoobey doobey-do," Dan replied.

"Dan, did you speak to Lilly?" I asked.

"Ohbedoobe–dooohha," was his reply.

"All right," I said. *Too many questions, I suppose?*

"Dan, you can light up in here. Did you hear they're going to have a singer in here tonight?" I asked.

No answer. Dan was taking out a cigarette to have with his coffee. He didn't appear in a bad mood but was in one of his no-answer zones. I'd learned how to live with them over the years. I just had to ignore them.

Now Dan was doing his Rain Man imitation of sipping a cup of coffee. Back and forth he went. No sooner did he drop the cup down than he would pick it back up for another sip. This went on for a good two minutes. I would just sit there watching, never quite able to stop looking.

Dan was dragging on his generic cig, making faces of displeasure when Big Tony came back. Apparently, Tony had the floor behind the counter built up, as he was at least another five inches taller again.

"Oh, well, every inch counts," Tony said. Tony placed his pack of Marlboros on the counter, and I knew that Dan was going to ask for one.

"Can I have one of your ciggies, ahh--?" Dan asked. He had forgotten Tony's name.

"Sure, Danish, help your self to the pack."

Tony took a long drag off of his dying butt. That drag was all that Dan needed to see to get him reaching for the pack.

"So, Dan, we have poetry recitals here every Sunday night, and although this is Monday, you're more than welcome to go up there after our singer does his set."

My brother started to go off on a poem that he was winging from the top of his head:

"Santa Anna, the words
And the desire to get your famous coffees.
Gee, thin wizzy
A sack of tomatoes
His pants are lasting without you
A free, free design of tomorrow
Boats and superior ducks
Bosses' coffees Banana delight!"

I gasped when I spied Tony's reaction.

"Whoa, Dan, that was good," said Tony. "You've got to go up there later."

Dan was all smiles.

"I've never heard one quite like that before. I think that you can be a hit here with that kind of stuff," said Tony. Dan's smile grew even bigger.

"Hey, listen, Steve, what do you guys think about this alien thing?" Tony asked, as he leaned onto the counter, turning to me.

Dan answered, "Oh, yeah, all the time, all the time!"

"Yeah," said Tony, "I think it's true, too. I just wasn't sure about you guys."

"You know, Big Toe," I somehow said, "it was my brother that made first contact before me."

"Listen, guys," Tony said, as he leaned even closer to us, "you got to be careful around these parts, you hear? There are a lot of folks that don't want to communicate with this thing. I mean, I got a church that comes in here every Sunday after services and not a one of 'em has ever mentioned a thing about it! They're all rather straitlaced off of the cuff here. And I don't think any of them have ever spoken to it. If they did, they sure ain't talking about it or letting anybody know."

"You know, Big T, what they say, don't you?" asked my brother. "If you don't want it to, it ain't gonna talk to you!"

Big T stood there for a second and looked like he just digested a ten-pound steak.

"You're right about that one, Dan," he replied. "Anyhow, where you guys from? I've never seen you around these parts before, and you boys sound like you've got a damn Yankee accent about you."

"We're from J- Jersey," I stammered.

"Jersey, Jersey, Jersey," Tony repeated.

"No, Tony, there's only one 'Jersey' in 'New Jersey,'" I corrected.

"Yeah, there's people from around here that think you northerners are crazy or that you're all pulling some kind of great conspiracy, if you say that you've spoken to that thing."

"We've been noticing that for sure," I said.

"Guys, I've got to help Maria out with the tables. They're starting to fill up. I'll be right back," he said, as he made his way off to the kitchen.

A voice from behind me startled me, asking if he could have one of those smokes on the counter. My brother turned towards the guy and offered one of his generic brands to him. He took one.

"My name's Ronnie, Ronnie Mulligan, fellows."

He extended his hand to both of us, and we shook it.

"Pleasure to meet you, Ron. This is my brother, Dan. I'm Steve."

"Where are you guys from?" Ronnie asked.

"We're from New Jersey," Dan replied.

"Well, I'm from Oklahoma, originally. I used to work on the Blue Ridge Parkway, but I'm retired now. I'm singing here tonight. You guys staying?"

"Oh, yeah," I said, "I wouldn't miss it for anything."

"Good, guys. Good."

Ronnie lit up his cigarette and blew out a mist of blue smoke.

"So, what are you guys doing down here?" Ronnie asked.

"We're checking out the Antique Trail and decided to get away from that nuclear power plant up north before the attack."

"Oh, so you guys are from up there," he replied. "It seems like great timing on your part to get out of there before that happened, or else you had something to do with it."

Just then, another guy approached us with a guitar case in hand and slapped an arm around Ronnie's shoulder.

"Hey guys, this is Charlie, Charlie Sorbatino, my guitar player," Ronnie said while shifting his cigarette from side to side in his mouth. "Charlie here is from Philadelphia, aren't you, Charlie?"

"Yep, moved down here to get away a few years ago. Just couldn't take it anymore, you know? I was getting to the point where I wanted to start killing people up there," said Charlie.

"Yep, know the feeling well, Charlie," I said. "And what about yourself, Charlie, what do you do down here for a living now?" I asked.

"I'm playing guitar and singing now while I do a little carpentry on the side. I moved down here about two years ago with my girlfriend, her boy, and my mom. Couldn't be happier!"

Tony came back to the counter and greeted Charlie and Ronnie.

"Hey, my guys are here! How you guys doing tonight?" he asked.

"All right, Big Boy," said Ronnie, as his cigarette ash dropped to the floor.

"Well, why don't you guys set up now? I think we got a big enough crowd, fellows."

"Where you guys sitting tonight, up front?" Tony asked Charlie and Ron. "I've got one table left for you up there. Better go up there now and grab it," he said.

"Tony, I need a bottled water, please," said Charlie.

"How about you, Ron, you want a rum and cola?"

"No, I've been trying to stay away from the alcohol lately. Just give me a water, too."

Charlie turned to Dan and me and asked us to come

join them at their table up front.

"Yeah, you guys can boo us real loud if we sound bad," said Charlie.

"Sounds like a good idea," I said, as we followed them. I asked Tony for a diet cola and another coffee for my brother as we turned to go.

Charlie took the stage by himself first and played acoustic guitar, solo. He played AC/DC, Neil Young, Guns 'n' Roses, and Bob Dylan. The place had filled up with about thirty people. It had the feel of an old fashioned coffeehouse with a thin veil of cigarette smoke floating lazily above the tables. As Charlie played, there was a soft murmur of idle chatter going on. Charlie was pretty good. He then motioned for Ronnie to come up.

"All right, friends, I know that you've been waiting to see the main act here. Some of you full timers that come into Big Tony's Town Square have gotten spoiled by this guy. So let's hear it for that sweet crooner, that Frank Sinatra sound-alike, that Bobby Darren, Mac the Knife, that one and only, Ronnie Mulligan."

The crowd applauded lightly, with a few hoots hollered in. Ronnie had a good voice. He sang many old standards and had the crowd singing along with many of them such as American Pie and Mac the Knife. You could see that this Ronnie guy had a stage presence. He was a real ham! Charlie played rhythm guitar behind Ron. At this point in time, Lilly appeared from seemingly nowhere and joined Dan at the table. She gave him a big hug and a kiss. She came over to me and gave me a little one.

"It's so great to see you again," I told Lilly.

"Dan didn't tell you that I was coming, Steve?"

"No, I asked him about your phone conversation,

but I guess that he wanted to keep it a surprise."

"Oh, I'm sorry, Steve. I asked him to see if it was all right with you."

"With me?" I exclaimed, "No, of course it's okay. You don't have to ask me, Lilly, no problem. It's great! Have a drink. What are you having? How about Dan? Does he need a refill?"

For the next half hour we sat together, Lilly close to Dan, listening to Ronnie and Charlie. Big Tony came over to the table and leaned over, ever so slightly, talking to Dan. He stood up, went over to, and greeted Lilly. They exchanged pleasantries. It seemed like they knew each other, considering Hibishaa was only about forty miles southwest of Canton. Charlie and Ronnie finished their set and joined us at the table. Tony then pulled himself up onto the stage with all of his might, as it was hard for him to get the right leverage with his short legs.

"Whew," he whistled a few times while trying to catch his breath, as he grabbed on to the microphone stand for some added support.

"How about a round of applause for Hibishaa's finest, Ronnie and Charlie? Thank you, guys. If anyone else is interested in coming up to the stage tonight to entertain us, please do. It is open mic from here on in. Welcome to the Town Square. That's right, it is the Town Square, and that is what country folk did in the olden days, they spoke up in the Town Square. Don't worry; we keep everything a secret here. The jail is closed for the night, so it's too late to lock anyone up for a bad performance, hahaha," he laughed, as his stomach rolled up and down with each bellow.

"Anyway, ladies and gentlemen, we are all in for a special treat tonight, as the Town Square is honored in having a special guest in the house. He may not be famous, and he may not be well known, but he is here tonight with us. Let me welcome to you the poet laureate, the Borscht-belt Milton Berle. Here he is, Dan Dunish, the Poet Man!"

The audience clapped. I looked on in disbelief. I looked over at Lilly, who was watching Dan stand up to get to the stage. She was applauding for my brother too. I stood up quickly to help Dan mount the stage. He had some difficulty with me, but got a few laughs as he was fighting my assistance with his left hand. Once onstage, he did a few of his Charlie Chaplin shuffle-steps, which immediately drew a large level of laughter. I backed up to my seat, almost missing it completely as I remained riveted on Dan. I felt as if I was dreaming this. As soon as he leaned over the microphone, which was now in its stand, Dan picked up his corduroy pants from both sides, and pulled them up about ten times in rapid succession in order to make sure that they were about three inches short of his chest. This immediately elicited a loud roar of laughter from the crowd and some people almost fell out of their chairs.

I couldn't believe what I was seeing. It felt like I had just woken up on the couch with the TV on late at night and was trying to focus my eyes on a late night TV host. Even Lilly was laughing.

Okay, I thought, *at least she's digging it!*

Charlie leaned over to ask me if Dan was a poet and where he picked up that schtick.

"Yeah," I said. "For about thirty years now. Where he picked it up," I repeated, blankly. "He's a natural. Just a natural, I guess."

In all of those years, with over one hundred poetry

notebooks written, not once could I remember Dan ever reading me one of his poems. He would always make me read them out loud. Half of the time, I couldn't decipher his writing, and neither could he. And now he was on stage without a poetry notebook.

Oh, my God, I thought, *I can't bear to watch this.*

"Hey," Dan said. "What did Burger King say to Dairy Queen?"

"What?" I heard someone call out from the crowd.

I cringed.

"You want to have a little burger!"

Half of the crowd laughed.

I thought to myself, *Oh, man!*

"Hey," my brother cried out to the audience, "what did the drill sergeant say to his troops?"

"What?" I heard another instigator in the crowd call out.

"Everybody get down! Hey..." said my brother, "I used to be a waiter in the Catskills. I used to serve soup to nuts!"

This got a laugh, too. Dan was on a roll. All that I could think of was that he was a braver soul than I. Dan was living out his dream.

The laughter died down, and Dan took on a more serious look as he drew closer to the microphone.

"Now," he said, "I'd like to give to you some of my poetry."

I waited, thinking, *How is he going to do this?* Ronnie leaned over, telling me that my brother was pretty funny, while laughing. I nodded my head in agreement. *Come on, Dan*, I prayed. Dan picked up his pants a few hundred more times, bringing another roar from the tables. Then he started:

"A lonely guy and a lovely misery
a mirror like a window
and a house with no chimney
red pants and a fancy dance
this is my liberty"

Dan went right into another poem:

"Shocking dad, proud ma
peephole Tom
boppin' John
I'm a con, run, run, run.

People started laughing and applauding. I was now in a state of shock.

"Strange intervention
New invention
Old interpretation
Imperial divination
Strange interpretation
People's appreciation."

"Next one, folks," he said:

"There's nothing to do tonight
Why don't we go to a bar
Blues rendezvous
Long line of lonely blues
I travel alone ever since I left home
thirty-five years ago
Long line of lonely blues
Traveled alone a long way from home
Florida to Utah and further
Down a highway of no return
Sun for awhile and then days waxed in one

Coke machines don't have a sign
Just a smile and no reply
Money is not to burn, only turn your ass, baby."

People were applauding now, loudly hooting and howling.

"Last one," he said:

"I have a window open at night
My hotel is warm, but my body is not
I don't even have a phone
My life is on loan
Please leave me alone
I'm all grown, and my beard is full
Tired of all the glum and bull
All of it makes a mystery."

Dan stopped. People stood up and gave my brother a standing ovation in downtown Hibishaa, West Virginia, the very first place that he ever took the stage. Lilly rushed up to the stage to hug and help Dan down. Before she could get him, he was doing his little jig steps, being the showman that he was while giving his audience an encore.

I stood up from my seat in total shock but found tears running down my cheeks, as my heart was bursting with happiness and love for my brother. He hadn't let me down once again. *Who is this guy?* I murmured to myself. Sometimes, just once in a while, Dan could convert to his old self. I'd seen it before, only a couple of times, once when my father was dying and Dan made phone calls in order to secure a second opinion for him. All of a sudden, he became the "old Dan." At times like these, I could still see that faint glimmering star, shining weakly, behind the cloudy milky way of his universe.

"How did you do that, Dan?" I asked upon his return.

Dan only shook his head. Lilly gave him another hug.

"Dan, that was utterly fantastic," said Charlie. "You're the Henny Youngman of Hibishaa."

Later, we sat at the counter while Tony leaned over talking to us.

"Well, here's my phone number guys," he said. "Stay in touch with me, will you? And Dan, the stage is yours whenever you want it."

The Town Square coffeehouse was closed for the night, as Maria cleaned the tables behind us. We exchanged telephone numbers. Ronnie and Charlie were leaving. It was nearing twelve o'clock.

Tony leaned over the bar once again, to talk to us. "You know that this alien thing has everybody worried." It's not so much that we're worried about this alien but more about those people that think it is evil!"

"I know," Lilly said. "I think that is why we're so scared of the terrorism part that might occur because of it."

"Well, that is part of the reason why Dan and I left our town, to get away from that power plant," I said.

"Look," said Tony, "a lot of us accept this thing as really happening, because we've spoken to it, and it's almost like a long-lost friend. But tomorrow should prove to the world without a doubt that it's real."

"I don't know about that, Tony," said Lilly. "You and I know that the folks down here are doubters. They'll probably refuse to believe it, because they don't want to believe it."

"I think that you're right, Lilly," I said.

"What about you, Dan, what do you think?" asked Tony.

"I really don't give a crap," replied Dan. "I have enough to worry about in my own head."

"Okay," said Tony, as he clapped his huge meaty hands. "Listen, be careful out there. A lot of these people down here don't like change. They like to be left alone in their own world. So just watch what you say when you're out there!"

FORTY-NINE

We slept well that night at the Nightie-Nite Motel in downtown Hibishaa. Dan and Lilly took a separate room when we returned from the Town Square. My cell phone rang at ten AM the next morning and jostled me out of sleep.

"Steve, hi, it's me, Lilly. I hope I'm not waking you up."

"Hey, Lilly, what's going on?" I said.

"Steve, I left early this morning to go open the restaurant. I didn't want to wake your brother. I just wanted to check in with you guys and let you know that last night was fantastic. How are you doing?"

"We're doing fine, Lilly. Dan is still sleeping in his room, I think. I'll go wake him up now, if you want to speak to him."

"No, that's all right Steve. I'll call him later today after work."

"That was nice of you to come down here last night. Dan was real happy to see you." I said.

"I was just as happy," she said. "There's something about your brother. I don't know what it is, but I really like him. Just tell Dan that I said hello and that I miss him. Wasn't he fantastic last night?"

He was unbelievable, Lilly. I still can't believe that he got up there and made up that poetry, somehow."

"Well, I'll give him a call later. You don't mind, do you, Steve?" she asked.

"No, Lilly, not at all. I think that it's the best thing that could've happened to Dan, him meeting you."

"Oh, great, Steve. You take care, brother."

She hung up. *She called me brother! Or did she ask me to take care of my brother?* I wasn't sure. Once again, though, she ushered in feelings of my deceased sister, Carole. Why did this lady have this effect on me? She was already treating me like family.

I went to Dan's room and knocked on his door. There was no answer. I strained to listen through the door to hear if he was moving around or if the bathroom water was running. Nothing. I knocked again for another minute, to no avail. I tried to smell if he was smoking, but the air conditioner was running, and I could not smell anything. I knew that Dan was a sound sleeper, but I was concerned. I took Oogie from my room and walked over to the motel office. I had the clerk come with me to open Dan's room. Once we arrived there, we tried knocking again. No answer. The clerk slid the master key into the lock, and the tumbler clicked. She opened the door slightly, while I called my brother's name out. As soon as the door budged open, we were hit with an overwhelming cloud of cigarette smoke. There at the kitchenette table sat Dan in his boxer shorts with a Marlboro in his hand.

"Dan," I said," are you okay?"

Dan didn't say anything as he smoked his cigarette with indifference, clouds of smoke billowing over his head, and piles of meds on the table. He did give me a curt look, though, whereupon he rolled his eyebrows up while shaking his head no.

"All right, you're fine, then," I said.

There was no use in communicating with Dan at times like this.

"I was just worried about you, since you didn't answer the door. Lilly called to say hi and that she'll call you back later today," I said.

I hurried outside to get the newspaper to see if there was any new proof given of the entity's existence.

There was none. I realized that it was still too early in the day for such news. Later, Dan and I sat at a table in Andy's Diner again, this time for a breakfast-lunch. The news was full of yesterday's stories regarding the historic world meeting. There was wide speculation as to how this order of proof was to be forthcoming. Dan was in a much better mood now, talking to me again. The world was repeating the alien's words of advice. "Watch time! In time! Time is relevant!" What did this all mean? He would show us today.

Dan was still grooving on last night; I could see it in his manners this afternoon at the diner. After thirty-five years, he finally felt a sense of accomplishment, a reason to live, a reason to feel good. He also had a girl in his life. How about that one? He was also spectacular last night. I didn't know how he pulled it off, but he did. Dan's mood had drastically changed since this morning's communication lapse. He now had a jump in his step, a twinkle in his baby blue eyes and a gift of gab that couldn't be turned off. He always talked when he was feeling good.

"Dan, how did you do that last night?" I asked.

"I really don't know, Steve. I just got up to the stage remembering two lines of the first poem and from there it took off. The rest came naturally to me."

"Well," I said, "it was great, Dan. They were great poems. Your jokes weren't bad either, kind of like a Shecki Green style, but your poetry was beautiful."

"Thank you, Steve," Dan replied confidently.

We got into the van around one-thirty in the afternoon and headed out of town southwesterly, down Route 21.We stopped at Slim Jim's Sunoco gas station to fill up. I took out my Wal-Mart USA Atlas to get my bearings straight. From the look of the map, we were about one-quarter of our way into the state. I was going to follow Route 21 for about seventy-five miles today, until I got to a town by the name of Liberty. There I would take an intersection off of Route 21 in order to get to a national park called Mountain Top Outpost.

I turned to tell Dan about my plans, but he was opening the door to find the bathroom. I thought that this would offer us an opportunity to try out my new generator for outdoor camping, again, since I didn't expect this park to have any electric hookups.

Dan came back with the news that he couldn't pee.

"What's there to worry about?" I asked.

Dan looked at me skeptically.

"I can't go," he said again.

"We have the pee container, Dan. You can go in that in the van. Listen, I plan to camp out tonight in a park."

"Do we have to go? Do we really have to do that?" Danny asked.

"I want to tryout the new tent and use the generator at least once on this trip, Dan."

"Why don't we just get another motel room?" he begged.

"We'll see, Dan, we'll see. We only have a few hours left for antiquing, so I'd like to get going before it's too late."

"Can we stop for some lunch and coffee real soon?" he asked.

"You've got to be kidding me, right? We just sat for an hour and a half at the diner and had breakfast. Come on, let's get a move on," I said.

I got Dan a super-sized coffee at Slim Jim's and finally headed off. It was a beautiful summer day in

West Virginia, the kind of day that was eighty degrees and never too hot. We saw many out-of-state RV-ers on the road antiquing like us. We turned on the radio in order to hear any news about the impending alien proof, but there was none. We drove by many garage sales that were usually too small to stop for. I got to thinking, though, that these garage sales were the best places to find something of value, since many a home owner was clearing out his or her house for more room and likely to pay less attention to worth. So we stopped at three garage sales, but had no luck.

We did hit upon two rather large flea markets along the way, where Dan bought another old poetry book. I ran around each market searching for paintings but did not find any more Renoirs.

"How much did you pay for that, Dan?" I asked.

"I got him down to five dollars."

"Not bad. What's the date of publishing on that book?" I asked. Dan handed the book over to me to find the year.

"Not bad, Dan. This is an old book, published in 1919. Apparently, you have found another genuine antique. At least one of us is doing well on our antique search," I said. It was now nearing five-thirty, so we continued on toward the town of Liberty. I soon found the turn at the intersection, and we headed towards the national park. I estimated that we should only be within thirty miles from there.

Not a word yet, about the entity's promise. I spent time flipping from station to station, but no proof was mentioned. It was hard to get a good station in these parts. The local stations seemed uninteresting, as country and religious music droned away on the airwaves. When they did have their hourly newsbreaks, they would give news on the local front. I asked my brother if he had heard anything from the entity today. But his only reply was to "give it time." Once in awhile I would get the feed on a good radio station, such as a national or a public broadcast, but it would soon fade out in mid-sentence to dissonance with every turn of the road.

The landscape was now changing. No longer were there towns and houses along the road. It went from farmland to pastures, to rolling hills and then to woods. Up ahead I saw a signpost in the distance. I slowed down and put on my eyeglasses. It said, "Weeser Town Limits." That was a relief for the moment. Signs were usually a precursor for something bigger ahead. Now a house was coming into view. There were soon three houses in a row. I hit my brakes until I slowed to a crawl, hoping to speak to someone for directions. As I peered off to my right, I could see that these homes were in disarray. They had personal possessions all over their front lawns. In fact, this appeared like the best yard sale of the day, except for the roots and the rust that accompanied them, growing out of the ground.

I knew from the past that this was just a way of life for these folks, a way of life vastly different than what most people were used to. Apparently, they had no storage sheds or available space in their backyards for these relics. There were washing machines, dryers, old cars, couches, chairs, swing sets, and clothing in piles. I thought to myself, *Would it be a good idea to make piles of clothes into compost? Maybe that's their idea?* This was no yard sale! Not by a stretch of the imagination.

I had spoken once with a fine young West Virginian one day while camping in a remote campsite in the foothills of the state. He had warned me to never stop at these types of neighborhoods. "You see," he said, "most of these people do not take well to outsiders, not even to fellow West Virginians. If you happen to break down in one of these areas, it would be wiser to just kiss yourself goodbye, because your cell phones don't work down here and they don't accept MasterCard!"

Whenever I would pass one of these Shangri-la's, there were usually men with ZZ Top beards in their overall jeans peering under the hoods of late-model cars. He warned me that I could disappear and my car would become parts on their front lawn. "Don't confuse this place for a used car lot out in the countryside."

I reneged on asking for directions and figured that we had another five more miles to go until we came to our destination. Five came and went. We did pass what I thought was a small factory, but at second glance, it had a high barbed-wire fence around it.

"Well, Oogie," I said, "maybe I ought to stop and check out the map?"

Just when I thought that I couldn't take any more driving, the road took a deep curve to the left and then veered into a clearing. We suddenly passed over another road with an entry and exit ramp. Not too far ahead on the right hand side was a small deli and convenience store. It was called the Quik Stop. There were three, maybe four cars in the front lot.

I found a spot towards the side of the store so that Oogie could take a much needed walk. When I returned to the van, Dan asked me to get him a decaf and some Camels. I was more than happy to get out for a break in the driving.

"I'll be right back," I told Dan. I needed to ask

directions to find this Mountain Top Outpost Park.

As I climbed on to the front steps of the porch, I could see inside of the front window. It seemed like a normal type of store, similar to ours back at home. I entered, setting off that jingling of bells announcing an entry. It was busy for a small place. Then again, there was nothing else for the past thirty miles that I had traveled. People were stopping in from work on their way home. Surprisingly, they all appeared to be in a New York state of mind-rush. It was uncommon to see small town folk move so fast. I felt out of place, since I wanted to stop the procession of activity and ask for directions. I purposely sauntered around the place, waiting for my chance to jump into an empty line at the register.

I checked to see if there was fresh decaffeinated coffee. The coffee burners were turned off except for one lone pot of remnant brew. I leaned over to sniff it. It was burnt from some time earlier in the day. I noticed there was a small deli section toward the back. I watched two young women of Asian descent scurrying behind the counter. Neither could speak any English. I turned to look at who appeared to be the proprietor, a middle-aged man of Anglo-American breeding. My calculating mind led me to believe that this was more than an interesting scenario.

This proprietor, though I envied him for obvious reasons, had a wild head of hair that hadn't seen the likes of a barber for many a year. He was bald in spots, an ex-hippie of sorts, lengthy on the shoulders, and gangly all around. He fit well into this area of desolation. I couldn't help but wonder to myself. *What kind of a relationship is he having with these two out of place women?*

My mind was racing like a two-ton horse. He wore those thick-rimmed, oversized, dorky, black-framed eyeglasses. His plaid shirt was way too tight and stretched across his out-of-shape, overhanging belly, with two buttons undone. It was stuck half in and half out of his baggy, creased corduroy pants, which were held up by a tattered black belt that extended a good foot out of the last belt buckle. He topped off his wardrobe with a pair of black oversized scuffed shoes, giving off a resemblance to a demented, dismissed, traveling circus clown. *Enough of my assessment!* I needed information, and there was now a break at the register.

"Hi, how are you?" I mustered up with all the sincerity of a slinking hyena. He had the nerve to look at me in an odd way. *Can you believe it? It must be the "how are you?" That's probably not customary down here!*

"Can I have two packs of Camels, filters, please?" *Crap*, I thought. *I said please!*

For some reason unbeknownst to me, this man was looking at me with disdain. *Maybe*, I thought, *I should go into my slight southern drawl. That's what must be wrong. He can tell I'm not from around here. Well, too late for that. I'll just have to be my normal self.* He put the packs of Camels down on the counter and said four- seventy-five.

I asked him if he knew where Mountain Top Outpost was.

He looked up at me kind of funny again.

"Why?" he asked. "Who wants to go there?"

I was perplexed at this reply.

"Me," I replied.

"Which way you headed?"

"I'm going this way," I said as I turned and pointed to that side of the road outside.

"Well, you went past it about five miles back. There's a sign for it right by the county jail. Did you see the jail?" he asked me.

"Yes, I think I did. That was the place with the barbed-wire fence around it?" I replied.

"Yep, that it was. If you go back there from here, you make a right turn after the jail to the park. It's a rough road, about three miles going up. You got a four-wheeler?" he asked.

"Nope. I have a conversion van."

He then chuckled three times, snickering to himself.

"Well, I don't know if you're gonna make it," he said smugly.

"Okay," I said, as I handed him a ten-dollar bill for the cigarettes.

He was going in the register for change when he asked me, "Just what are ya doing up there anyways, huntin?"

"No," I said, "I'm just looking for a place to camp for the night. I saw on the map that it was a national park up there."

"Nah, it ain't no camping up there, 'cept for hunters. There ain't no park rangers and no hookups. It's primitive camping. Are you from around here?" he asked me.

"Nope," I said, "just traveling through."

"I didn't think so!" he said. He gave me my change.

"Are you packing?" he asked me.

"Packing what?" I replied, confused.

"Are you carrying?" he questioned. I still didn't get it.

"Do you have a gun?" he asked, as he chuckled again.

"No, just pepper spray," I said.

"Well, that will ward off a charging squirrel," he said.

I could hear the sound of giggling, now coming from the line behind me.

"All rightie," I said, "what's wrong with the place?"

"Do you remember about three years ago of a mass killing up there in these parts? It was all over the national networks. There were these three hikers on the Appalachian Trail that stopped in that campsite for the night. Theys were hiking the whole trail from one end to the other. These local hunters were up there for the night, and theys got to being pretty drunk and messed up. Ya know what I mean? Theys decided to rape the two girl hikers every which way while they made the guy watch. Then theys stabbed all three of them and skinned 'em, leaving them hanging in the trees for the next days to come. It was a brutal scene when they found em!"

I stood there in disbelief. I could feel a cold chill running down my back. *We ain't in Kansas anymore, ain't we, Alice, I thought. This sure ain't Disney World.*

"Well, on second thought," I said, "I'll take your advice and skip it. I think that I do remember that happening. So where can I find another campground around here?"

"Let me see. Your best bet would be at the Riverside Trailer Park about a mile down the way you were heading, on the left- hand side. You'll know it if you passed it, because you'll come to a bridge on the left taking you into the town of Radner. I think they even got some RV hookup sites down there," he said.

"Well, thanks for all the advice," I said.

I realized that there were two local patrons standing in line behind me, both looking like they were two of the mountain top killers. As I left, I could feel their eyes peering through me as the two Asian girls giggled to themselves behind the deli counter.

After that encounter, I left the store feeling a bit uneasy about the area. I was starting up the van, sitting in the driver's seat, when the front door of the Quik Stop jarred open real sudden, and out popped one of those ruffled-looking patrons who were standing behind me in line. He bolted down the front steps in one leap and hit the ground running straight at me. *Oh, God*, I thought, frozen behind the steering wheel. He came right up to my window and handed me the two packs of Camels that I had left behind on the counter.

"Thought yer might a wanted these, hah," he said, handing me the smokes through the window. I know that my eyes were popping out of their sockets and that my mouth was hanging open then as I reached for the smokes and replied, "Thanks, man!" I don't know why I think crazy thoughts at times like these, but at that moment, I thought, *I'll bet these guys don't listen to Jim Cramer on Mad Money much? I'll bet they don't!*

FIFTY

Dan was staring oddly at me.

"What happened in there?" he asked.

"Oh, nothing," I said. "The guy told me a story."

"A story about what?" Dan asked.

"Oh, just that the camping up there is not any good, so we're going to try a trailer park," I said.

"Can we get something to eat soon, too, Steve? I'm starving."

"Well, it's six-thirty now, so let's get a campsite first, and then we'll go into town to eat," I said.

"Always the boss, always the boss," Dan mumbled, just loud enough for me to hear. "Okay, Hitler," he said emphatically.

A mile down the road we turned into the Riverside Trailer Park. It was located on the banks of the Schnugel River; at least that's what I thought it was called. It separated us from the town on the other side, which I took to be Radner. We rode around the trailer park in order to check out the best spots left for camping.

"Seems to be flooded in many areas close to the riverside," I told Dan.

"Steve," Dan said, "why don't we just get a motel room in town?"

"That might be a good idea, Dan. Let's check this out first."

We drove the perimeter of the park. This was a permanent housing arrangement for most of the occupants. They were living in old '50s-style trailers that no longer had tires under them. Most of these residents seemed like "lifers" from the look of the old, rotted items that lay strewn on their properties. They did not appear to be "moving up the ladder," so to speak, as there were a few of those, too, lying broken in pieces on the ground. Not a soul was stirring outside. Their cars looked like junkyard relics, with dents, rust and faded paint.

We could smell dinners cooking as we passed each trailer. By the end of our circling, we came to the park office, which should have been condemned but somehow got past their town's housing inspectors. This office was the smallest of all the trailers we had seen so far and was attached to a broken down shed, Lil' Abner style.

"Stay here, Dan, I'm going inside," I said.

I had to step around an old red Ford pickup truck from the '60s. I entered a dark, dingy room filled with cigarette smoke and the stench of stale beer. I couldn't make out anything after stepping inside from dusk to no light at all. I stood still for fear that I would walk into something.

"What can I do yer for?" was the first thing that I heard, accented with a heavy southern twang.

My eyes finally adjusted and settled upon an old school desk at which a skinny dude was sitting. He appeared to be in his late twenties. Once again, my crazy mind took hold of my better senses and begged me to ask him where the local Jewish Temple was in town. I immediately shrugged off that urge. Behind him and off to his left was another room with a couple of guys drinking beers inside.

"Hey," I said, "I'm looking for a place to park my van for the night."

"Ya need a hookup?"

"Yeah, I can use electric," I said.

"Well, that's all we got raht now, just electric, no sauer and water," he replied.

"That sounds all right," I said. "What do you get for that?"

"That'll be twenty," he said. "It's site number twenty-two."

"Isn't that the one with the old Chevy next to it?" I asked.

"Yep, dat's da one," he replied.

"Well, I'll take it," I said.

"Ya gotta fill out this piece of paper heere first," he said.

He gave me a form that asked for my name, phone number, address, type of vehicle I was driving and the license plate number. I gave it back to this skinny guy, and he looked it over, turning it upside down and sideways, like he was looking at hieroglyphics.

"Now, dat's Shipprow, yer last name?" he asked.

"That's close," I said. "It's Shapiro."

He said it over, about three times before he got it right. Each time was painful to witness.

"Shapearoooh, Shaparooh, Shapiro? Wut kinda a name is dat? Is dat Juwishh, or sumpin?" he asked.

"Nahhh," I answered. "It's German."

"Yer German," he repeated, a bit surprised.

"Yup," I replied, "good old German and part natural American, can't yer tell?" I said.

Went too heavy with that southern drawl just then... I hope that he doesn't kill me now! He peered at me kind of funny for a few seconds, through these small bee-bee eyes that he had, squinting them at me in that dark room.

"I ain't never herd of a name like dat one before!" he said. "Yer from up dere in New Jersee?"

"Yup, good old Jersey," I said, quite uncomfortably.

I gave him my twenty, and he fished around in the

desk for a pen and piece of paper. He ripped it in half and scribbled something illegible on it for me. I looked at it and shoved it in my pocket. The other two guys behind him were cracking open more beers. They called out his name—Wiley-- and asked him if he wanted another.

"Yep," he said back. He turned back to me. "Yer got anyone wit yer?"

"Yup," I said. "I got my brother and my dog."

"Okay, dat's oohkay," he said, after taking a swig of his beer.

"Yer staying fer just one night, raht?"

"Raht," I said back.

I did it again. I must have a subconscious death wish, I thought. He kind of looked at me funny. I figured then that I better lay off of the drawl if I wanted to see daylight tomorrow.

"Listen," I said, "are there any places to eat around here?"

"Welp," he said, while dragging on his cigarette, and probably thinking that some raht poisoning might right now just suffice for me, "Ders dat food mart up da way, an ders da Radner's Inn in town." He then blew the smoke my way.

"All rightie," I said, "Thanks." I stepped back outside.

"Geez," I said to Dan as I climbed back into the van. "I don't know about these guys! We got a spot to stay for the night, so let's go into town to eat."

We made a left-hand turn and headed towards Radner. We crossed over the Schnugel Black River into a perpetual ghost town. We were suddenly jolted by the horn of the Great Appalachian Southern Railway as it echoed its presence through the speaker box valley that we were in. The never-ending serpentine slid along, with its grinding metal wheels and that " clickety-clack, clickety-clack" chorus, resonating in our ears.

The Radner Inn sat parallel to the tracks of the Great Southern and remained the focal point of a dead town. It stood four stories high with boarded-up windows above its entranceway. There were three cars parked outside of the inn as we pulled up. I fed Oogie his dinner in the van and then went inside with Dan.

The building had a sign posted on top of its archway stating, "Circa 1855." Below it was another sign saying, "Authentic Italian Food." We stood inside of a massive empty lobby. There was a bar toward the back with a television playing, so we headed that way. Off to our right-hand side was a dining room where three families sat, quietly eating.

"Dan," I said, "Let's sit at the bar so that we can hear the TV. Also, please let me do the talking here, because I'm a little bit concerned about these people here, okay?"

"That's fine with me," said Dan. "Can I smoke in here?"

"There's an ashtray on the counter, so it must be okay to smoke," I said. Dan lit up a Camel. A man of slight build came through the kitchen doors to greet us. He looked to be in his fifties, with a neatly trimmed mustache.

"How can I help you gentlemen tonight?" he asked.

Before I could speak, my brother uttered, "Whatabawhatbawhatbaluuuu," to my surprise. This man put his head forward and raised his eyebrows in amazement at my brother's remark. Quickly I asked if we could see two menus.

As he turned to get two menus, I stared at my brother, who in return just shrugged his shoulders at me.

"Are you trying to get us killed here?" I asked in a low voice.

"Oh, so you had to take us to a dangerous place, hah, bright boy?" Dan responded. The bartender gave us two one-page plastic menus with seven items listed on it for dinner. That was it, no more and no less. *They must have been running out of Italian tonight?*

"You guys want a table?" he asked.

"Nah, is it all right if we eat here at the bar?" I motioned to it.

"That's fine with me," he said as his moustache twitched.

Dan needed something soft to eat because of his lingering acid reflux, so we both ordered the meatballs and spaghetti dinners. The television was on low, but we could still hear it as a news brief broke prior to the eight-o'clock show. The newscaster mentioned in her report that, as of now, there was still no proof given of the entity's existence. Since this was a local affiliate of the broadcast station, there was a twinge of "I told you so" in her voice. The bartender had also been watching the newscast from the side of the bar counter while smoking one of his own cigarettes.

He turned to us and said, "I always knew this was some kind of a piece of crap. It's those Communists in this country! Those damn people who only want to make money. When we find them we should kill them all, damned traitors. I just can't figure out why they're doing it this time."

I looked at Dan and said in a very low voice, "Not a thing, don't say a thing." I then responded out loud,

"You got my vote, my friend."

The bartender continued to drag on his smoke. I could hear him mutter under his breath.

"It's always for money, always for money. Those Commie bastards."

He came over to us when he brought our meals out of the kitchen. I prayed that he hadn't sprinkled our sauce with rat poison, after my brother's audacious greeting and since we were new to the area. By now, I had lost my appetite but knew that this wouldn't be the type of place to waste food.

"Yeah," I chimed in, "I never believed in any of this."

"Nobody around these parts has ever spoken to this thing! They would be crazy if they did. That's why I think it's some type of big advertising thing that they're doing for a movie or something, or it's them damned terrorists trying to scare us. I wish we could find somebody to drop bombs on or hang. It makes me so mad that I want to go get my shotgun, and shoot someone."

"That's a good idea," I said wholeheartedly.

FIFTY-ONE

"See what I mean about these parts, Dan?"

"Yeah, Steve, why the hell did we ever come down here in the first place?"

"I don't know, Dan. Sometimes I think that I'm just crazy."

It was already dark when we backed into our camping spot. I took Oogie out for a final walk around the park. Outside, not a soul stirred. I could see the flicker of lights from the TVs that were playing as we passed by the trailers. Oogie and I came upon the park office with the red pickup truck parked in front. Sitting nearby were the same three guys from earlier, except they were much more inebriated. There was no doubt about their condition, as they made disparaging, sometimes indiscernible remarks as I proceeded on by. I thought that I could hear the words "effing something bastard," but I wasn't certain. Then I heard an empty beer can hitting the ground behind me. I pretended not to hear it, and kept on walking.

Dan was sitting in a lawn chair next to the van, smoking a cigarette when I returned with Oogie.

"All right, Dan," I said, "I'm going to plug in the electricity for the night so that we can have lights and heat."

I had decided that I wasn't going to upset my brother with what had just transpired on my walk. He already had enough on his mind. It was turning out to be a comfortable night with no rain in the forecast. I figured that it would get down into the forties, though, so it was a wise choice to have the electric heater on in the van.

"Listen, Dan," I said, "As inconvenient as it may

seem, you're going to have to smoke outside tonight, because there's just not enough room in the van for it."

"All right, Steve," Dan replied from outside.

I put up the front window curtains for our privacy. We were all set for a much needed night of rest.

"Why don't you give Lilly a call tonight?" I asked my brother.

"That's a good idea," he said.

"Here, let me dial the number for you," I said.

I waited for the dial connection, but the phone would not work. I looked down at its window only to see that it was in a non-serviceable area, emergency calls only.

"It won't work here, Dan. Lilly's probably tried to call you, too, and can't get through."

"We'll call her in the morning," I heard my brother say.

I started up the engine in order to run the television. Reception was always poor wherever I camped, since I only had an inside antenna. I did manage to get a Spanish station that came through very clear. My understanding of Spanish was minimal, though. *Why*, I wondered, *are Spanish stations the only ones that came in clear? Ahhh, one of the mysteries of life.* I did pick up a West Virginian affiliate station of channel three that was fuzzy but audible.

Once again, the news reported no new proof of the entity's existence and that its time limit of 12AM was rapidly approaching. I opened up the side door of the van to let my brother know that we were going to have to share the bed inside tonight, since I did not want to set up the tent with those nutty guys running loose.

Dan was smoking one of his cigarettes while I was sitting inside with Oogie at my feet, reading my book, when I noticed a car going by. It had slowed to a crawl and then stopped in front of my vehicle. I stood up immediately and opened the side door to see who it was. It hastily took off, though, leaving me looking at the back of an old pickup truck.

"What did they want?" my brother called out to me. "They were laughing and cursing at me."

"Dan," I said, "why don't you climb back in the van with me? We'll figure something out about smoking in here."

Once inside, I turned off the engine and the TV and lowered the lamp to dim. I looked at my watch, which showed it was eleven- fifteen.

"Okay, let's wait to see if they come back," I said.

We sat quietly, staring in each other's eyes. Oogie was sitting up with us, feeling our tension.

"What was that?" Dan said, as something moved around outside of our campsite.

In the total silence, I could hear it scratching against the van.

"It sounds like it's moving around the van," Dan whispered.

We strained our ears to listen.

"I don't hear any voices or footsteps, Dan. Maybe it's just the wind or a tree branch rubbing against the van?"

"Maybe they dropped someone off to get us?" Dan said.

We both jumped from our seats when we heard the loud horn blast of the Appalachian Southern freight train as it started its passage through the valley. Every five seconds, the engineer would blast his horn, for whatever reason I couldn't imagine. The metal wheels of the train screeched bloody mercy into the night, with every churn repeating its grinding chorus. This was a freight train straight out of hell. *How could these people ever sleep at night?*, I wondered. Our attention was temporarily diverted from fear to squeaky uneasiness. At this point in time, I thought it would be wiser to get out of here.

"Listen, Dan," I said. "I've had enough of this."

"What were you waiting for, Einstein," my brother replied, "someone to tell you to leave here?"

"We have to wait first for this train to pass," I said. "Let me go outside to disconnect our electric and get ready to go."

The train had finally passed, still rumbling and shrieking its horn in the valley like some deranged kiddie dragon ride at the seashore amusement park. I climbed outside of my van, leaving my door open. I stood silently for just a moment to take a quick look around. My eyes took a few seconds to adjust in the darkness. Nothing. I couldn't see anything out of the ordinary. *Okay*, I said to myself, as I started to tiptoe around the van.

I did not see any over hanging branches that would have been scratching against the sides. As I passed around the back, I stopped, frozen in my tracks. I felt like something was just around the corner. The hairs on the back of my head were tingling. I leaned over slowly to peek around the passenger side of the van. No less than two feet away from me, camouflaged and arching its back, a junkyard cat jumped straight up in to the air, scaring the bojangles out of me. I let out a scream as the cat did the same, while vertically launching its body with feet sprawled apart. I quickly pulled the plug out of the electric hookup and reeled it back into the van. I ran back to my driver's door and got back in.

"Okay," I said, out of breath, "It would be better to

leave now then to wait for them to come back here again. But we're going to have to sneak out of here. I don't want to drive past their office, so I'm going to go in the opposite direction from which we came. I'll keep my lights off."

Dan sat speechless while I turned on my ignition. I licked my lips, as they suddenly grew parched. I did not touch my gas pedal for fear of being heard. Silently we pulled out. I hit my lock button on the door, making sure that all of the doors were locked. Dan was sitting up front with me, staring outside for any headlights moving around in the park. If they were to come, they would be heading our way. The glow of the moon led us through the trailer park and up toward the exit ramp. I turned left to go up a slight hill to the highway. I did not want to hit my brake lights upon entering the road, so I listened and looked for any oncoming headlights and then slowly coasted on out. I headed into the direction that I had come from earlier in the day, figuring that I knew this way better than going the other way. I hadn't noticed that we were driving with our headlights off until we passed the Quik Stop grocery mart on our left. I threw them on.

"Whewwww," I bellowed out in relief. "It's a good thing we got out of there, Dan."

"I'm going to the back for a smoke," Dan said, as he climbed over Oogie to get there.

"Maybe we can get a motel room for the rest of the night," he said.

It sounded like a good idea to me. Too bad that I hadn't listened to my brother before.

"Well, we got about thirty miles to go in order to find one," I said. "Why don't you lie down and try to get some sleep?"

"Are you going to be all right driving, Steve?" Dan asked me.

"I think so, Dan. Thirty miles is about a half hour's worth of driving. Let's see, it's only twelve o'clock now," I said.

I flicked on the radio in hope of finding some news about the alien's promise. *At least this is an easy drive*, I thought to myself. From what I could remember about this afternoon, it would be a predominantly straight drive. There were no streetlights on this road, but our journey was aided by the yellow glow of the moon. No sooner had I relaxed into a comfortable sitting position than I noticed two distant headlights in my rearview mirror. I hadn't passed one single car and therefore rationalized that it was a bit unusual that someone else would be driving behind me at this time of night in Radner, West Virginia.

Forget about the news, I thought, as my concentration was now zeroed in upon the careful observation of those headlights behind me. *How could it be those guys from the trailer park?* I thought, as my eyes darted from the road to my rearview mirror. *It could be anyone else. I'm just worrying myself to death. Could they have seen me leaving? They may have driven by our campsite once more, only to notice it vacant.*

I kept staring out through my side and rearview mirrors. This car was gradually drawing closer. I would lose it temporarily over small hills and slight turns in the road, only to see it return as quickly as it disappeared. Still, my inner fears were telling me that this car was trying to catch up to me.

Dan was lying on the sofa, while Oogie was asleep on the floor. I decided not to say anything to Dan. I checked my speedometer. I was traveling at sixty miles per hour. This car had to be going at least five miles faster, on a lonely country road at twelve-fifteen in the morning. That was going pretty fast in my book. But then again, I was always told how fast these country people drove down here in order to get from one town to another. Perhaps such was the case? I didn't like the idea of going any faster in a conversion van on a dark country road with the possibility of a deer crossing in front of me.

What would those three drunken lunatics be after me for? Was it because I was from New Jersey? Could they tell that I had spoken to the entity? Or did they not like my brother, my last name, or my fake drawl? *I didn't say anything out of line to that guy*, I thought. *This can't be them. How could that old pickup move so fast? But what if it is? These idiots are drunk and liable to do anything.* After that story I was told back at the Quik Stop, how could I be sure of anything? Those hunters sodomized and raped the two females. They made that poor guy they were with watch in horror. Then they knifed, gutted, and skinned all three of them, only to leave them hanging in the trees like deer carcasses. What reason did I have to be scared? Meanwhile, they were getting closer and I didn't know what to do.

I reached quickly for my cell phone while trying to keep my eyes on the road. I flipped it open. I could see that the screen was still reading that I was in a dead zone. But it did say no calls except for emergencies. I dialed 911. The phone rang once, twice, three times and then went dead. I did it again, only to get the same result. I threw the phone back down in my cup holder. I looked back in my rearview mirror. To my horror, they were closer now and had their high beams on. I could only estimate they were less than a mile behind me.

I had to do something. I decided to turn off my lights while driving. The light from the full moon was bright enough to faintly see ahead of me. I looked up again in my mirror. There was no sign of them. Then I realized that I was coming out of a turn and that they were again closer. *What are the chances that these are the guys?* I thought. The chance was far too great to take. There they were again, gaining. I wondered if they could see my van with my lights off. I suddenly felt the need to do something fast. I kept peering out to the sides of the road for a clearing or a place to hide my van. I realized that I would have to slow down even more, in order to make certain of seeing a possible turnoff. My estimation was that they were approximately thirty seconds behind me.

I approached another bend in the road with a deeper pitch than before. I did not want to touch my brakes, fearing they would see my tail-lights. I took my foot off of the gas pedal to coast down. As I did, I saw what appeared to be an abandoned driveway, quickly coming into view on my passenger side. Since we were on a bend, I realized that they could not see me, so I hit my brakes as hard as I could. The van went into a slight fishtail, and the tires squealed. Clothing and pillows from the overhead storage flew forward on to the floor, waking Oogie and Dan from their slumber. Dan was grabbing on to the sides of the sofa for dear life and saying something, while Oogie was thrown into the front console. My only chance now was to take this turn at about five miles per hour. I turned sharply, hitting gravel and hedge bush as my tires skidded out. The hedge bush was thick enough to cushion my slide and held us upright. My back wheels grabbed traction and shot us forward. I immediately stopped the van, took my foot off of the brake, and turned off the ignition.

I figured that we were a good thirty feet into the abandoned driveway. I looked into my rear view mirror to see if they were still coming. My brother asked me "What's happening?" I could not answer. My heart was in my mouth. I saw the beams of the vehicle coming around the bend. It grew brighter as it filtered through the branches around me. I could hear the sounds of its engine growing louder, unmistakably a truck. I could see it as it shot by in my mirror. It was a pickup truck.

FIFTY-TWO

Oogie was up and standing next to me, wagging his tail. I checked to see if he was all right.

"Are you all right, boy? I'm sorry, Oogie. Let me see you."

Thankfully, he appeared to be no worse for wear.

"That was them," I told Dan, as I turned to see his ghost-white face.

"Well, what are we going to do, Steve? I'm pretty scared," he said. "What do those guys want from us?"

"I don't know," I said. "Let's think what we should do."

Dan lit up a Camel.

"Now, we can stay put right here and hide," I said.

Dan inhaled and blew out smoke nervously.

"What if they come back and find us?" Dan said.

"Then I'd say we're in pretty big trouble. We can back out of here now and head back in the opposite direction, but I'm pretty scared of that idea, too," I said. "Or we can continue in the direction that we we're going. But what if they pass us coming back?" I lamented. Dan was speechless as an ash dropped off of his cigarette and fell onto the carpet.

"I'm pretty sure it was them," I said. "I mean, they were going pretty fast past us, and I can't be one hundred percent certain that it was their pickup, but it was a pickup! How many pickups would be traveling out here at this time of night?"

"I'm scared, Steve."

"So am I, Dan."

"Why don't you call the police?" Dan suggested.

"I'll try it again," I said.

I grabbed my phone and dialed 911 again. The screen showed "NO SERVICE, emergency calls only." Then I tried dialing zero. The phone began to ring on the other end but was disconnected after three rings. I turned to look at Dan.

"It won't work," I said remorsefully. "If they saw us up ahead in the road when we had our lights on, then they probably knew it was us. After I turned my lights out, what would they be thinking?"

Dan had no answer for a while.

"Well, I think they would turn around eventually, Steve."

"I agree, Dan. So here's the deal. They turn around thinking that we pulled off somewhere, but they have no idea where. Plus remember, these guys are half lit. So they may check every dirt road and turnoff that they know of on their way back. That's the scary part."

"All right," Dan said as he took in a deep inhale of his Camel.

"Maybe they'll just give up or miss some spots."

"True, Dan. That's why I think we should just stay here and try to move the van farther up in order to camouflage it. If these guys are as drunk as I think they are, they're not going to see us if we're hidden pretty well back here."

"All right, Steve, whatever you think is best."

"Let me see if I can hide us any better," I said.

I took my flashlight and stepped outside. It was cold. The temperature out here in West Virginia must have dropped down to forty degrees in the middle of the summer. The air had a fresh, clean smell to it. Oogie was pressing against the front passenger window, begging to join me.

"I don't know if you should come, Oog," I said.

He looked at me with his omniscient eyes. I couldn't resist him.

"Are you going to stay with me, boy?" I asked. "You have to stay with me, okay?"

I let him out. He went off to the brush to sniff and relieve himself. *All right*, I said to myself as I turned the flashlight in a three-hundred-and-sixty-degree circle. I walked part way down the abandoned driveway, which had tall grass all about. I estimated that I was about fifty feet from the roadway. I paced myself back up the driveway and realized it went another twenty feet and then veered off to its left. I could now make out that this use to be a circular driveway. The circular part continued through a heavy thicket of vines and brush. *This might be a good place for hiding*, I thought.

I shined my light to see if the van could fit into this space. I went back to the van to get my work gloves. I put Oogie back into the van, which was just one less thing to worry about. As I was clearing away brush, I thought that I caught a glimpse of something. I turned my flashlight back on and shined it through the dense underbrush. Sure enough, there in the middle of this lot were the remnants of an old farmhouse. Its roof was sheared off, while its walls were collapsed. The structure was reduced to a pile of debris sitting on a cement foundation. I turned suddenly, hearing the hoot of an owl somewhere above me. I thought to myself that this might work.

I began to remove more branches and thicket. After a good fifteen minutes, I climbed back into the van, started it up and began moving forward slowly. I had to back up two times in order to navigate the circular turn. I could hear the paint on my driver's side getting scratched and scraped as I squeezed her in. I didn't care too much about it at this point in time.

I stepped outside once again and inspected that side of my van. I was going to need some heavy compounding, since I could make out the peeling paint and scratch marks from hitting the brush. I backed away from my van a good twenty feet and turned off my flashlight. I could barely see my vehicle. I walked further down to the beginning of the driveway and turned my flashlight back on toward my hiding place. I could not see it. I next looked around the driveway for any tire marks, which I found and then hurriedly erased them with my shoes, smoothing out the ground. I went back to the van. Dan and Oogie were both happy to see me again.

"All right," I said, "I think we'll stay here for the night."

All three of us huddled in the darkness, too scared to turn on a lantern. It was now around one in the morning.

"Steve, I've got to go."

"Go where, Dan?" I asked.

"I've got to go number two!"

"Oh, no, Dan. Can't you hold it?" I begged.

"No, I don't think so, Steven."

"All right, Dan. Let me grab the flashlight and then come with me outside. Take your sweater, too. It's cold."

We stood outside of the van, shivering.

"Where am I going to go, Steve?"

"Well, take off your pants and underwear. Here, let me get your shoes off."

I took Dan to the rear of the driveway through a small clearing, naked from his waist down. I had him put his shoes back on, unlaced. He then followed me to the back.

"Ouch, ouch," he said, as he stepped through some underlying brush.

"Where, Steve, where?"

"Dan, go right here," I said, as I handed him a roll of toilet paper and turned to leave him for some privacy.

"But there's no place to sit, Steve! How am I going to do this?" I heard him say.

"Dan, you're going to have to do this standing up, so bombs away! Spread your legs open, Dan."

After that episode, I turned the radio back on, real low. Dan was sitting comfortably in the side chair smoking a well-deserved Camel. I found one of those national public radio stations.

"You know what else is strange today, Dan?" I asked.

"No, what?"

"There was no proof given by the entity," I said.

"I know," said Dan. "I can't even talk to him today."

"That's too bad. I wonder what's going to happen now?" I asked. "I just thought of something. I better go out to the road to check if we can be seen from the other direction."

"Aw, come on, Steve, don't go out there again," Dan pleaded.

"I've got to, Dan. I can make out the road from our position here, so I need to go out there and check. I'll be right back," I said.

With that said, I stepped out of the van with flashlight in hand and headed down the driveway on to the road.

Okay, I thought to myself, as I walked a good one hundred feet past our hideaway. I shined the light from the road into the woods looking for my van.

I was satisfied that I couldn't make it out. There was no way that a passing car could see us. Even as I walked back up the driveway, I could not see the van parked behind the brush. I was content that we'd be safe now. It had been a half hour since we entered the abandoned driveway and no cars had passed by, except for the pickup.

I was about to step back into the van when I heard it. I wasn't sure, but I strained my ears to listen. It was intermittent at first. When the wind was blowing, I could not hear it. When the wind died down and the air laid still, that's when I could make out the sound. It was certainly growing louder. I thought it might be the sound of an engine, but I wasn't sure. My instinct led me back down the driveway and onto the road. I crossed to the other side to see around the curve, but all was darkness. I turned quickly back toward the other direction that we were heading in, in time to see the narrow dots of the headlights coming my way from far off. I bolted across the street and ran back up the driveway. As I jumped back into the van, I was breathless once more.

"Damn," I said, as I slammed the door shut.

Dan jumped up from his seat and stared at me with terror.

"There's a car coming from the other direction," I said.

Dan leaned over from his side seat to gain a look through the windshield. We could see the lights growing stronger as they projected weird images through the trees. I could only hope that I had been too far away from this vehicle to be seen. Perhaps they would have mistaken me for a deer from that distance? But what about my flashlight? I couldn't remember if

I had left it on. What if they had seen that? If they did, we were in trouble. Meanwhile, that vehicle was bearing down upon our hiding place. We could clearly hear the rev of the engine. Our van became lit up inside, as if the night was turning into daylight. They were right upon us now, as we both watched this automobile zoom on by. Luckily, it was not a pickup.

A minute or two passed before we spoke.

"Okay," I said. "I think we're going to be all right now."

"You know what they said on the radio when you were outside?" Dan asked.

"Nope, why don't you tell me?" I asked my brother.

"They said that they found the proof that the entity left," he said.

"Get out of here," I said. "What was it?"

"They said that yesterday, Tuesday, was changed to Wednesday!"

"Wednesday," I repeated. "What are you talking about?"

Dan was getting mad. He did not like to be misunderstood. He took it as a personal affront.

"All right," he said, "don't believe anything that I say!"

"Dan, I do believe you. I just don't understand. How can that be?"

Dan repeated that Tuesday was changed to Wednesday, yesterday.

"Oh, my God," I said. "How can that be possible?"

"I don't know, Steve. Listen to the radio."

I waited for the next newsbreak on the public radio station. Sure as Dan said, scientists watching our atomic clocks were the first to discover that our time was off by exactly twenty-four hours. It had moved up one day into the future. Doubting their readings, astronomers from the World Board of Physics and Astronomy were called upon to check their data with the positioning of the stars. After close scrutiny by all major telescopes in the world, the Board confirmed their findings. Soon after making this discovery, the entity assured them that this was in fact, true. World leaders were perplexed upon hearing this news yet decided to keep the days in the week the same, as if nothing had changed.

"It would be easier to adjust our astrological charts than it would be to skip a day," they agreed. "This would remain our simplest solution".

Although this incident was taken by most world leaders as definitive proof of the entity's existence, dissidents still believed this to be a hoax, perpetrated by evil capitalistic nations of the world. The entity had maintained that it would never be able to provide sufficient enough proof to some. When questioned as to why it caused such a dilemma with our time, the entity responded that its hope was to show some type of tangible, physical proof that could be seen and tested by all. Meanwhile, the governments of the world had now posted red alerts in fear of possible terrorist actions.

FIFTY-THREE

Dan and I must have dozed off. I remember hearing the radio playing while sleeping. I had the strangest dream. I dreamed that Dan and I were hiding out in this abandoned driveway in the middle of nowhere. All was peaceful at the moment. God only knew, we needed the rest. I could here the entity talking to us through the radio.

"Well, did you like my proof of time, Steve?"

"Yes," I could hear Dan saying, as I turned to see him talking in his sleep.

"It was the best I could do," said the entity. "You know that I can only contact you in certain ways, don't you?"

I was about to say no, when I heard my brother again say no, while he was still sleeping.

Then my cell phone rang. I was startled, since I couldn't call out in this area. I was hesitant to pick it up. Surprisingly, neither my brother nor Oogie heard the ringing. Both lay completely still, like corpses. I thought that I must be going crazy, but then again, I realized that I was probably still dreaming. I looked around the van. I noticed that someone must have turned the lantern off. The phone was still ringing, so I flipped it open while reaching for my eyeglasses. With my glasses on, I could see that there was no name or phone number showing from my phone contacts for this call. *Should I answer this?* I wondered. My brother called out in his sleep, "Answer the phone!" I hit the talk button.

"Hello?" I said in the deepest male voice that I could muster up. I always thought that a deep man's voice helped to intimidate the other caller. There was no response on the other end. I could hear their phone then click, similar to when someone is trying to hang up on you. I stayed on the line and I could hear them pick their phone up again to see if I was still there.

They must have had that very old-fashioned type of phone, you know, that rotary kind. I said again, "Hello, why don't you speak to me?" This time they stayed on the line but still didn't talk. I held my breath. My brother was still sound asleep on the bed. I looked outside of the van windows, wondering if this was at all real. The night outside was pitch black. I reached over to the console of my van for my watch but surprisingly found it void of all numbers, dials, and time. I then glanced up at my dashboard clock, hoping to find it working, but it, too, was blinking incessantly, with four dashes and no time showing. Then I heard a voice.

"Why don't you just hang up?" asked the entity.

"Well, I think I will," I said.

"You wouldn't believe who that was if I told you," said the entity.

"What do you mean by that?" I shot back.

"That was a loved one from your past, Steve."

I didn't say anything, but I thought to myself, *How could that be*?

"Oh, there's a lot that could be," said the entity.

I must be dreaming this. I could never get a call from a deceased loved one. Impossible, just impossible!

"Well, yeah, it's impossible for them to speak to you, but they do get through sometimes with noises or in dreams," said the entity.

"Come on," I said out loud. "I'm dreaming this now."

"Yes, you are dreaming this now," said the entity.

"But your phone really did ring. All that I'm actually saying is that your dreams are not that far off from what you call reality. You believe that your conscious state is the only state that is real. There is so little that you know."

"So you're saying that my dreams are real contacts with my deceased loved ones," I said.

"Yes, I am, and the dream is like the telephone for communication," said the entity.

FIFTY-FOUR

Oogie woke me from my slumber. I heard his barking from afar. It grew louder and more incessant as I regained consciousness. I opened my eyes from my sleeping position on the floor, as I was lying on my back staring at the ceiling. The radio was softly playing in the background. I lay still, thinking that I was still dreaming. Then I noticed a feint light bouncing upon the walls of the van. The light became brighter, as it lit up the interior of the van, gradually. I sat up quickly. Oogie was standing next to me, barking toward the rear of the van. I turned to face the back, which was the portion of the van that was angling out from our hiding place in the driveway. I looked back again at the dashboard of the van to see that the digital clock was now flashing four-thirty in the morning. Except for this light that was intensifying, the outside was still pitch black.

I said to myself, "Oh, no," as I fumbled on the floor for my flashlight. I wondered if I was still dreaming.

I could hear my own breathing, heavy and labored. What the heck was going on? I had remembered that I was dreaming before. *UFOs?* I thought. *This is all about UFOs? What the heck is a UFO doing here now?*

My brother called out in his sleep, "Not now, go away!"

I was petrified. I sat in fear, holding on to Oogie as his barking became snarls and his hairs stood straight up on his nape. I could now see the light taking shape as a glowing ball and coming toward the rear of the van. I could make out what I thought was the crunch of footsteps as this glare became blinding. I couldn't see anything in the van and believed that we were about to be accosted by some thing or those guys! The last thing that I remembered was my brother jumping up and screaming at me, "What is that thing?"

I must have passed out, because I found Dan leaning over me and asking if I was all right. There was a loud banging on the driver's side of the van. I got up to look, although I was shaking from fright. There was what appeared to be a face staring in at us. Oogie was across in the passenger's seat, barking ferociously. I stood up upon weakened knees and angled myself closer to that window. I didn't know what made me move closer to have a better look, but I couldn't tell if I was still dreaming. The glare of the light made this face appear more grotesque, similar to one on Halloween night. The banging continued and forced the van to rock from side to side.

"Who is that?" I yelled.

The figure moved its face flush up against the window. The light was suddenly turned off, casting a monstrous shadow upon the glass.

"Sheriffs Office," he said. "Open up your van!"

FIFTY-FIVE

"Please speak to me! It is very important. This is Norman. I'm at the NOMAD Command Center, and it's critical that we talk."

"Norman, I'm here," answered the entity. "I know what you're going to ask."

"It wasn't good enough," pleaded Norman. "We need better proof than that."

"I don't know what else I can do, Norman."

"Why can't you just appear? A picture is worth a thousand words, you know?"

"Yes, I know," said the entity. "But just as I have explained it to your scientists, I do not exist in your physical world."

"My friend, we're begging you to please try once more. President Smith has been informed by our Secret Service that a serious attack is imminent if you are not proven authentic. Our reports show that it is likely to happen soon and that it will be massive. Please, my friend, can't you try to prevent it? The rest of the world is under tremendous tension, between believers and nonbelievers. Riots are happening right now in the streets in such places as Rome, Paris, Tokyo, and all over."

"Well, Norman, I warned you from the beginning that this type of reaction would be expected."

"But friend, you also said that no harm would befall us!"

"I still maintain that, Norman. It will be of no difference whether I prove myself or not. Your fear is overriding my trust. Your world will not believe that I am real, no matter what I do."

"This attack is planned to happen within twenty-four hours, your entity."

"Norman, as I have told your world before, no harm will befall you."

"Oh, just one other thing, friend. The President has asked if you could please switch the days back to what they were previously."

The entity laughed. "I can do that Norman, but I won't!"

"Why not?" asked Norman.

"This, my friend, shall remain forever in your pious, superficial world. For now, you are another day older, and hopefully, another day wiser!"

FIFTY-SIX

It was close to eleven when I awoke in my van. I had the windows closed, and the heat was stifling. I didn't remember much about where I was. I did remember, though, that we had followed the sheriff all the way out to Route 21 late last night. It seems that he had noticed the tire skid marks on the road, directly in front of the abandoned driveway that we were holed up in. He told us that those trailer park guys were always up to no good.

I turned on my ignition in order to open the windows. I took Oogie out for a much needed walk in the fresh air. After returning to the van, I grabbed his bowl from inside and filled it with water. This truck stop was abuzz with activity. I found myself parked between two big rigs, and the truckers were not pleased with that. On my way back to the van, I received many a honk from their air horns, since I was occupying one of their premium parking spots. It was lunchtime, and these truckers were circling the rear parking lot like a flock of vultures, seeking a space.

I climbed back into the van with Oogie and moved out to the front of the truck stop where daily commuters and travelers like myself parked their cars. As I left, I received a few foreign salutes, better known as the finger, as a dangerous game of musical chairs erupted for my spot. Dan was now stirring in the back bed.

"Where are we?" he inquired. "I've got to pee real bad and take my meds, Steve!"

"We're in a truck stop," I said. "There's the pee bottle right over there. We stopped in a truck stop last night, and that's where we're at right now."

As Dan took care of his business, he asked me what happened last night.

"Don't you remember?" I asked.

"Well, kind of. I remember hiding out and then waking up with that light shining in on us. Then there was that cop. I was scared to death," he said.

"Right," I said. "We followed him all the way out to route 21 and then pulled into here. He had said that he knew those guys chasing us and they are always causing trouble. Let's go inside and get some breakfast, Dan. That's one night I would like to forget."

We went to the men's room to wash up and then found two seats at the counter area with the truckers. The place was packed. Our waitress Mary took our order, and all was fine until she asked Dan what he was having.

"What are ya having, hon?"

"Ohhh, I'll have something soft and gooey," he said, loud enough for all of the truckers to hear.

One of the truckers barked out that he would like one, too.

"Oh, we got a real joker here," said Mary.

I slowly lowered my head into my hands, knowing what to expect from here on in.

"Okay, so what it'll be, honey?" asked Mary again.

"Something nice, and soft and gooey, please. And I'll have a Sanka, too," answered Dan.

"All right," Mary said, as she leveled herself against the counter for balance. "So do you want some eggs, hon?"

"Yeah, I'll have some eggs," said my brother.

"And how would you like them, aside from all over your head?" she asked.

This comment brought a great uproar of laughter

from the truckers, as some started chanting, "Go, Mar, go, go, Mar, go." I looked at Dan to see how he was handling the situation. He was not perturbed in the least and appeared to be deviously enjoying this game.

"Would you like them scrambled, fried, over, over easy, soft boiled, hard boiled, or what?" asked Mary.

"Soft," said Dan.

That's all that it took. With that, all of the truckers at the counter fell into stitches. A couple of guys laughed so hard that they came off of their stools and walked away to catch their breath. At this point in time, I thought it only fair to intercede and to help Mary out. I knew that my brother would continue this barrage of torment, relentlessly. I had seen it done in the past.

"He'll have three eggs over easy, whole wheat toast, home fries, and a decaffeinated coffee, please, Mary," I said.

"What are you guys, a comedy team or something?" Mary asked me as she was jotting down our orders.

"Yeah," I couldn't help myself from saying. "We're Schmergeggy and Maghee and we're traveling the world."

Then Mary made the mistake of asking me which one of us was Schmergeggy and which was Maghee, and I told her to ask my brother. On that note, Mary turned around and headed toward the kitchen after I heard her say something like, "Oh, crap."

My brother turned to me and thanked me. The truckers were still in an uproar, as once it got quiet, one would break off into hysterics and the others would follow suit. One guy had his coffee shoot out of his mouth and across the counter.

I turned to my brother and said, "You're a real comedian." But I knew that the act wasn't over yet, not by a long shot. I knew my brother too well; I just waited.

"I'm sorry," said the guy sitting next to me. "I just can't stop."

"That's okay, don't worry about it," I replied. I turned again to look at my brother, whose hair had seemed to have grown another two inches straight up and out since last night, giving him the appearance of a bad hair day for Don King. I laid my chin down into one of my hands on the counter and just sighed.

"Are you okay?" I asked Dan.

"Yeah, I've got to go out for a smokie," he said.

"Oh, boy," I said to myself. "Here we go."

Dan stood up in his particular Dan fashion, gingerly grabbing the counter many times, adjusting for support, and then lifting his corduroys right up to his chest line a few hundred times. It kind of reminded me of a seagull standing next to you on a hot balmy day at the beach, flapping his wings a hundred times but never taking off. I didn't have to look. I simply held my chin in my hand and stared blankly ahead at nothing. I waited. Soon I could hear the attempts of muffled laughter again, beginning to rise. He grabbed on to the back of his swerving counter stool in order to gain some temporary balance. I said to myself, "Here we go, here we go."

Dan plucked his cap on to his head and then proceeded to do that patented cha-cha-cha two-step, moving back and forth, similar to a blind man doing the Michael Jackson moonwalk. It took awhile before he finally put it into first gear, and then he shuffled off. I didn't have to wait any longer. Most of the truckers had to get up and leave the area because they were laughing so hard. When they returned, most had tears in their eyes.

Dan returned in time to get his breakfast while it was still warm. He savored the coffee. Up and down the cup went. When you thought it would stay in the saucer, it was just a mistake in judgment. Up it would go again six, maybe seven times.

I looked at my brother and remembered when he was a normal guy, a regular brother that I always adored. I admired and loved him even more for what he'd dealt with, but still. *Why did this have to happen to him?* I wondered, as tears welled up in my eyes. I was the stupid one. At least no one would have noticed the difference if this had happened to me. He could've been taking care of me, living high on the hog as a lawyer. The trucker next to Dan asked him if he was a driver, too.

"Oh, yeah," I could hear my brother say. My brother had never driven a car in his life!

"What are you guys driving out there?" asked the trucker.

"My brothers got a big old Dodge," said Dan.

"Oh, yeah, and what are you hauling?"

"Oh, we're hauling chickens, chicks, chicks, chicks," Dan repeated.

"Chickens," the trucker echoed.

"Yeah, chickies, that's what we got," Dan said.

"Where are you hauling from?" asked the trucker.

"Ohhhh, we're from New Jersey," said Dan.

The trucker then looked at Dan quizzically, while scratching the side of his head.

"What's your handle out there, in case I want to talk with you guys?" he asked Dan.

"Oh, we're Big Hand," Dan told him. "Really, Big, Big, Big Hand."

I was now peering sidelong at these two, not believing this conversation. I honestly didn't care anymore! My brother could tell him whatever he wanted to. This was turning into fun.

"So, you drive too, Big Hand?" the trucker asked Dan.

"Oh, yeah, I do most of the driving," my brother said.

I could see the trucker grimace and roll his eyes back after Dan said that. *Oh, this is a good one*, I thought. Then I was sure that I heard the trucker mumble something like, "New Jersey drivers." This was turning into a much better day than yesterday, or whatever day it was.

After eating and hanging out for about two hours, we were back on the road and headed down Route 21. I had checked the map and saw that Green Bank, West Virginia was only fifty miles away. Green Bank was the one place that I wanted to see on this trip, more than the Antique trail. Green Bank was the destination of the NRAO, the National Radio Astronomy Observatory. I had been there a few years back and was intrigued by their mission and presentations. They were the organization that started out by searching the heavens for radio contact for other life, SETI.

Later they took part in many other valuable scientific ventures and experiments of observations, such as surveying the invisible parts of the universe by means of radio waves. Being an avid astronomy and physics buff, I couldn't help but wonder what their thoughts would be about our alien visitor. Not for that reason alone, I wanted to attend one of their presentations again, hoping that they would touch upon this matter.

FIFTY-SEVEN

"Steve, can we get a motel room tonight? I don't want to sleep in the van again. I'll pay for it," said Dan.

"Okay, Dan, I think that's a good idea. We'll go halvsies," I promised.

We stopped at a few flea markets along the way. I picked up a painting supposedly by an Armand Desiree Gautier, an 1875 date on the canvas. Of course, I wasn't certain if it was a print or the original. I knew that the chances of it being an original were next to nil. More importantly though was that my brother looked around with me for a short time. This made me feel like 'old times', like those days in the Bronx. Upon leaving our final flea market of the day, Dan asked me if I had noticed that dark-haired mysterious lady again.

"No," I said, "Where did you see her?"

"Well, she pulled up in a car and parked right next to me in the van," Dan said. "At one of the flea markets."

"What kind of a car did she have?" I asked.

"Steve, you know me with cars! I don't know. It was a convertible, I think."

"Do you remember what color it was?"

"It was red, I think."

"And you're pretty sure that this was the same lady that you've seen before?" I asked.

"All right, Steve, don't believe me! I'm never right. I don't want to talk about it anymore," Dan said.

"No, come on, Dan, I'm sorry. I believe you. I'm just trying to figure this out! Work with me, man!"

"Yeah, I'm pretty sure of it," he said. "She had the same sunglasses and baseball cap on."

"But Dan, if she's following me, why would she be parking right next to the van knowing that you might be in there watching her?"

"Maybe it's just a coincidence, Steve, I don't know. Do I look like Perry Mason? But I do know that she was following you around again."

"Why didn't you come and get me, Dan, and tell me?"

"Well, I don't have wings! I was smoking a ciggie in here and she walked away so quickly behind you that I couldn't have caught up if I tried. Do you have any more questions, Your Honor? Dan asked.

Just then, my cell phone rang and scared the heck out of both of us. It was Lilly. I gave the phone to Dan. I wasn't certain if my brother was imagining this lady in sunglasses, but for the most part when I had doubts, he turned out to be right. It could purely be coincidental, just as he suggested, but what were the chances of that? Many people travel the same routes during the Antique Trail days and often cross paths more than once. In fact, I heard that many an enduring friendship have been made by these encounters. I couldn't tell if this lady was really following me. The only thing that I knew was that this trip was far more than I ever bargained for. My gut feeling though, was telling me that I was being followed.

The rest of the afternoon passed by rather quickly, and before we knew it, we were driving into the town of Green Bank, West Virginia, the home of the National Radio Astronomy Observatory. We were searching for a motel room when we happened upon the entranceway to the NRAO facility.

"Dan, let me go in here for a minute. I want to see if they're having any presentations today."

I came back in a few minutes with a schedule in my hand.

"They said that they were open tonight for a special gathering. Do you want to go with me tonight, Dan?"

"No, I'm pretty busy tonight, Steve! Just kidding! I'm really tired, Steve. I just want to go eat, get a motel room and hang out. You go, Steve. I'll be all right! This is the first night that my acid reflux is feeling better."

I went back inside to sign myself up for the show.

We found a decent motel not too far from the Observatory. It had a restaurant on the premises, which made it perfect for Dan. It was six o'clock, and we had enough time for dinner, feeding and walking Oogie, and then for me, getting back to the eight o'clock presentation at the NRAO.

Dan had me get him a couple of packs of Camels at the Piggly Wiggly down the street. He was all set up for the night. I was ready to leave when he started to cough again from his acid reflux. Apparently, it was from the dinner that Dan just finished that was too rich and was now causing the recurrence. The poor guy could not catch a break.

"Are you okay?" I asked.

Dan waved his hand, indicating that he was fine.

"Is there anything that I can do for you?" I asked. Dan shook his head no and waved with his hand that I should go. As I closed the motel door behind me, I could hear him coughing. I left him with his Camels and his poetry.

FIFTY-EIGHT

"Please come in," the lady at the register motioned. "That will be six dollars for the admission to tonight's show, please. Please find a seat in the auditorium. It's on a first-come first-served basis tonight."

I secured a seat in the middle of the room. I placed my windbreaker jacket over my chair to reserve it. I went out into the lobby to pick up a program for tonight's presentation but was told that there was none, due to the impromptu scheduling for this evening.

"Do you know what it is about?" I inquired with an usher.

"No, sir," he said. "I only know that our Director will be acting as the host tonight for a very special guest."

With that in mind, I wandered into the lobby to have a look around. All through the facility were amazing photographs and displays depicting the history of radio astronomy. There were radio wave images of the universe. There were pictures from a multitude of projects, analyzing our heavens through the use of the various types of radio wavelengths available. Radio waves gave a much clearer picture than did optical telescopes. It could see through clouds and obscurations that an optical telescope could not.

I stepped outside of the building in order to get some fresh air. My focus was drawn to the enormous GBT, or Green Bank Telescope, over one hundred meters in diameter. It stood four hundred and eighty feet tall, taller than the Statue of Liberty. It reminded me of one of those hideous Martians from *The War of the Worlds*.

The parking lots were filling to capacity. Soon vehicles were parking on the grass. Security personnel were turning back cars and the gates had to be secured in order to stop the overflow. I wondered if this was customary for a weekday show in such an obscure place, tucked away in the solitude and foothills of West Virginia. Through the main gates rumbled a motorcade of dark-colored vehicles with an escort of state police. I noticed many news vans with their broadcasting antennae hoisted high above. I assumed that something extraordinary was going to take place.

Upon reentering the building, I was lucky to have my ticket in my pocket. Ushers were now standing in place and examining all patrons for their admission stubs. I got in line and moved slowly down the aisle towards my seat, which I was grateful to still have. There was a feeling of excitement in the air, as the crowd actively conversed. I asked the couple sitting next to me if they knew what was going on. The lady turned to me and eagerly said that tonight had something to do with the entity's efforts to offer more proof to the world of its existence. I could have fainted when I heard that.

The lights in the auditorium dimmed on and off and then were lowered as the crowd quieted down to a whisper. On to the stage walked a lady. She was a person not fitting my stereotype of a scientist or a physicist. First of all, she was too well dressed for the role of the absentminded professor. With her hair perfectly coiffed, she elicited the impression of a Fortune Five Hundred executive instead of a disheveled astronomer. She was clearing her throat while adjusting the microphone.

"Ladies and gentlemen, it is truly an honor to

welcome all of you here tonight to the National Radio Astronomy Observatory. Tonight, ladies and gentlemen, you are about to embark on perhaps one of mankind's greatest events in history. You are the lucky participants in this monumental meeting for our civilization. It is with great pride that our agency has been asked to host this proceeding and to accept this request. We will be broadcasting throughout the free world tonight, and we must ask you now if you will be willing to be a part of this. If not, then you should leave the auditorium under your own volition."

No one stood up to leave.

"I am the Director of The National Radio Astronomy Observatory, Doctor Stephanie Lipus."

The audience did not applaud or stir. I believe that everyone was spellbound.

"We received a call earlier today from NOMAD, which stands for The National Organization of Military and Defense. Their acting Director, Doctor Norman Lewis, who is also our Secretary of Defense, had asked us if they could use our facility in order to assist them in a matter of worldly importance. The Doctor and I have been in discussion all day with the entity, our visitor from another world. With the guidance of the entity, we have been able to set up our telescopes, both radio and optical, along with many of the other major telescopes of the world to specific coordinates in the sky, in order to provide us with quite possibly our first visual image of our visitor. We realize how important an endeavor this is to our world in such a trying time!

"Our President, James Smith, along with other world leaders, has been requesting such visual proof to quell the rising tensions created by disbelievers through out the free world. With that in mind, the entity has agreed to assist us tonight. Ladies and gentlemen, you will be asked to help us in this endeavor. Your part is crucial. First and above all, your safety will not be compromised. Second, you will be asked to wear special head-phones that will enable you to participate in this operation. Third, the entity proclaims that even visual proof will not be enough to satisfy those whom refuse to believe. And finally, it wants you to know that without your help, seeing the entity would be impossible. Therefore, your open-mindedness remains a crucial ingredient to the success of our viewing of the entity.

"It is the energy of your mind that is most closely related to the entity's existence. The entity has already explained to the world that it is vastly different than anything known to man. In this context, it wants you to know that it does not truly come from outer space, as we call it! It comes from a deeper space, one not yet explored by us or even realized by us, that of our inner minds. The entity wants you to know that throughout human history, we have shown the ability to accept new notions and to adapt to them, such as the world being round, theories of infinity and that our planet Earth is not the center of all life. New concepts and discoveries have always been a part of an advancing civilization.

"The entity is more connected to our dream state while we sleep. That is when our minds turn off from the visual world around us and enter into the world that we know so little about. He, she, or it, has the ability to be in both worlds and can travel through both, as this is a connection that we do not share. It has entered our universe through our minds. Since we are such visual creatures by nature, it has decided to incorporate its appearance as best as it can from the mental to the optical. Ladies and gentlemen, our visitor has no real visual shape in our universe. But with the use of our headphones, our minds, and the telescopes available, he believes that he can recreate his image for our world to see.

"It is only normal for a civilization such as ours, in our infancy, to scour the skies for answers. We, therefore, should treat this event as an awakening for now as well as for the future. We must become aware that there is more to be seen than meets the naked eye," the exuberant Director proclaimed.

"Now, ladies and gentlemen, I must ask you again, if there is anyone who does not wish to participate in this experiment, please excuse yourself from the room." The room stirred in nervous conversation, as everyone looked around to see who would leave. Not a soul rose from their seat.

"I must ask you once again."

There was silence.

"I must then take this to mean that you are all willing participants! Very good. I want you to know that the entity itself will take over the next portion of this proceeding, ladies and gentlemen, and will be speaking directly with you. I must thank you now and ask that you please remain seated, if you can. If you have to leave the auditorium for any reason, we will not be able to let you back in. Your total cooperation and concentration is imperative for this to succeed."

FIFTY-NINE

The lights were dimmed to near darkness. The ceiling above lit up to reveal our stars and heavens. Soothing music began to play lightly in the background.

"I am still here with you," said Doctor Lipus. "I will remain here on stage during the proceedings. Please put your headphones on now."

Rustling could be heard in the background, as people fumbled with their headsets and the auditorium grew silent with anticipation.

"Thank you, ladies and gentlemen, for being here tonight and for being willing participants in what hopefully will be a monumental milestone for mankind."

I recognized the voice. It was the entity speaking. It was that same voice that I had become so familiar with, although I knew that everyone else was hearing a different voice according to their own liking.

"I will lead you tonight in our quest. I want you to relax. I will speak to you much like a hypnotist. I will bring you into total tranquility."

"You may be wondering if your presence here tonight was planned in some way? To a degree, it was. In fact, you are all here because you are all open-minded people. You may think that I brought you here, but you have brought yourselves. As noted by Doctor Lipus, I am a part of the mind. In regard to matters of the universe and life in general, I do not control fate. In fact, to the best of my knowledge, there is no such thing as fate, unless we have all been planned, preprogrammed and controlled by a superior being, one of whom I am not aware of. And that, my friends, would be a remarkable feat, even by our God."

"Please, let me continue. All of the maladies in your world today have been caused by your closed-mindedness. Your world is in peril due to your shortsightedness. But tonight I know that I have people who are willing to explore new concepts, along with new ideas, regardless of whether you accept them or not. And that is crucial for this visualization to succeed. With your energy, positive nature and the science of your telescopes, we will be able to show your world where I am and what I am."

"Ladies and gentlemen, you are hypnotized right now! Whether you believe that or not is of small consequence. You are relaxed. We are one and the same now. You are a part of me and I of you. Being one is the answer, because it shows concern for all."

"My mission is to enlighten you. Your first alien contact should be a revelation and a celebration of life. That is why I am trying to make your world believe that this is really happening. So tonight, with your mental assistance, I will attempt to accomplish that."

"At this time, ladies and gentlemen, the VLAs, which stand for the Very Large Array of telescopes in Socorro, New Mexico, have been positioned to zoom into a direct coordinate in the skies above. This same coordinate is being analyzed by the GBT as we speak, that is, the Green Bank Telescope, right here at this facility. Other powerful telescopes throughout the world are keyed into the very same spot. I will ask you all to turn your gaze to the ceiling above and to direct your attention to the brightest object on the left side. That is correct. It looks like a star. It is the one that is positioned next to the projection of earth. Please keep looking. You are totally relaxed and tranquil. Your minds are now concentrating on my exact location.

The computers are busy analyzing this position above the earth. Your concentration is aiding this information, as my location is being passed through your minds up to the computers. Now, as you can see, an image is beginning to appear in that very spot that we are affixed to."

I knew that I was hypnotized. I had been so once before, but this time I felt as if I was sleeping with my eyes wide open. I was maintaining my gaze at that twinkling star in the ceiling above. I could hear the entity as if he was standing behind me, saying that we were doing a great job. I could see an image taking shape from that twinkling object above me. It appeared as if it was something electric, cloudlike and effervescent. This image was taking shape right next to the projection of our earth. The earth seemed to be wavering and sparkling now as well. I could actually feel the room shaking, as if we were having a slight earthquake. Nobody in the audience reacted though, as they were glued in their awe with their mouths agape. Our whole planet was vibrant, encompassed by this effusive energy field.

The earth had taken on a form of wavering shapes, sparkling and tingling. I could actually feel an electric current running through my body. It was quite a pleasant feeling. I noticed that others around me had their hairs standing on end. I touched my own head to discover mine doing the same. The entity began to speak again.

"We now have a perfect image of what I would appear like in your dimensions. You may now move your eyes back to the stage. My presence has been successfully recorded for all of mankind and history to see. What other proof could you want? Will this also be considered a fabrication of the mind?"

Doctor Stephanie Lipus was now addressing us at the podium.

"Ladies, and gentlemen, our science and computer staff have been diligently at work coordinating and verifying all information received. It is their belief that all images seen were real and not fabricated in any manner. We have been witness tonight to a remarkable historical moment. We hope for mankind's sake that this will provide some solace and peace regarding the entity. We thank you for attending."

I raced back to the motel room to tell Dan what I had witnessed. I found him sitting quietly at the efficiency table smoking a Camel and staring off into space.

"Dan," I said, "did you see what happened on TV?"

"No," he said, as he exhaled a huge amount of smoke into the air. "I saw and heard the whole thing, just sitting here."

SIXTY

We were sitting in the Galaxy Diner in Little Nyah, West Virginia, planning our final leg home.

"Come on, Steve, let's just get home."

"I want to stop in one more place, Dan," I said.

"What's that?" he asked.

"There's a state park called Ten Gallon Hat directly on the way home in West Virginia that's supposed to be a beautiful place," I said.

"So, how long are we going to stay there?" asked my brother.

"Just for one night, Dan. I really want to try the new tent out at least once before we get home. Plus you can sleep in the van."

"Can't we go home today? Haven't we had enough?" he pleaded.

"Oh, come on, Dan, this is one of the most beautiful states in the country and the people are just fine here, except for those three guys that we ran into. Plus I don't think that we could make it all the way home by tonight, anyway," I said.

"Well, as long as we get home by tomorrow, Steve."

"Okay, Dan, that's a deal."

We pulled into the Ten Gallon Hat State Park around two. This seemed like the first time that we were taking it easy on our trip. I registered in the park office and took an electric hookup site.

"How many campers do you have in the park today?" I asked.

"Not that many, sir," said the park ranger. "I think that we have about three occupants right now, but two are expected to leave this afternoon, so you have the park to yourself. Why do you ask?"

"Oh, I was just thinking of getting a remote spot out by the lake if possible."

"That's not a problem. Here's the map. Here's where you're at, right here. Why don't you drive out this way and check out the sites. Come on back and let me know which one you pick."

I picked a site as close to the lake as possible for Oogie's benefit. It then took me a good half hour to set the tent up for the first time. I couldn't ask Dan to help much, but he did hold up one end while I fastened the other. Once that was done, I took Oogie for a much-deserved romp up the trails. As old as "Big Bear" was, which was his nickname, he still bolted ahead, acting as my scout. Every minute he would return, only to take off again to check a newer section of the trail. He had his bells on his collars, which acted as a deterrent to any unexpected bear. We hiked for a couple of miles until I knew that he was getting winded, and then we turned around and headed back.

Dan was drinking a diet cola and smoking a cigarette in his folding chair. Oogie caught sight of the lake next to our campsite and jumped in. I pulled up a chair next to Dan.

"Have you spoken to him today?" I asked.

"Yes, I've spoken with Herbie a few times," he replied.

"Herbie," I repeated, as I chuckled.

"Yes, that's what I decided to call him. It's a lot easier than no name at all," said Dan.

"I guess," I said. "I think I have to speak to him later. What did you talk about?"

Dan did not answer. He was into one of his moods again, for some reason. I sat quietly for five minutes before I stood up to go to the tent.

Dan called out, “Can we go to the diner now?”

“Well, yeah,” I said. “But I’d like to take a short nap if you don’t mind. If I’m not up in an hour, wake me by five-o‘clock.”

SIXTY-ONE

We left the park at about five in search of a place to eat. I wasn't certain which direction to go, so I stopped at the rangers' office to check with them. The office was closed for the day but did have a local map outside, attached to the wall. I could see that the closest semblance of a town was a little place called Cinderblocks, not too far from the park. I turned right and headed off in that direction. While driving thru the back roads, we passed a half-hidden sign in front of an old stately mansion that was in dire need of repair. The sign had wild brush and tall grass engulfing it.

"Dan, did you see that?" I asked, as we passed it by.

"No, what?" he asked in a rather displeasured tone.

"There was a sign back there that I think said, 'Madame DeFarge's Culinary.' Do you think that meant food, Dan?"

"Well, genius, the last time I looked it up in the dictionary, 'culinary' meant 'food,' Steve! Go back, Steve. The last time I had a brain, that's what it meant."

"Okay, Dan, since you put it so nicely, I think I'll turn around."

Dan mumbled something else, but I didn't bother to ask, somehow knowing that it was along the same lines of what I had already heard. I managed to find an abandoned driveway and maneuvered a nifty K-turn to head back. These country roads can go for miles before offering a place to pull over or turn around. I slowed down while approaching the farmhouse and came to a stop in front of the sign.

"Dan," I said, "you can't even see the sign from this

direction. I don't know about this one. Don't you think that we've gotten ourselves into enough trouble on this trip already?"

The place gave the appearance that it had seen better days and perhaps served its last meal over a hundred years ago. There were no cars around.

"What do you mean we've gotten ourselves in trouble, Steve? You've gotten us into trouble on this trip so far, Hitler! I think that this place is going to be fine. Why don't you pull into the driveway, big boy?" he said.

I just stared at my brother for a while. My mouth was feeling parched all of a sudden, and I knew that it was hanging open. Dan was purposely not looking my way.

"Let's go in," he said. "This one's on me."

"Dan, this place is in the middle of nowhere on an old country road. How could it be…"

"Just pull in, Steve. I have to go to the bathroom."

I turned into this dusty dirt road of a driveway looking around, not knowing why I was going along with it. I thought that I heard my brother mumble again, this time something like, "I thought that would get him to go!" Not a soul was stirring. Not even a sound, except for the crackling of my all-terrain tires going up the driveway. It was eerie. It was strange. It was a magnificent old colonial farmhouse from the Civil War era, with huge weather-beaten white columns surrounding a front and side porch. There were enormous elm trees standing stoically, as if on guard, protecting its glory and its past. Not even the wind blew. It was devoid of all sound.

"Dan," I asked, "what about the name of this place?"

"I know, Steve. It's Marie Defarge, from *A Tale of Two Cities*. Let me out," Dan said. "I have to go!"

I stopped the van perpendicular to a side stairway that led up to the porch and a side door. As Dan stepped out of the van, the side door of the farmhouse swung mysteriously open, revealing an old lady in a housedress, motioning for him to come in. I swore that I heard her speak.

"This way, Daniel."

I looked on in disbelief as I pulled my van over and parked it.

I was afraid to get out of the van. I told Oogie to be a good boy and that I would be back. I could see that this elderly lady was waiting for me, so I had no choice but to go. She was five feet tall, if that, and was wearing black, half-boot orthopedics, with withered opaque socks that hung down, looking like old stockings that a grandmother used to wear. She was working her mouth as if chewing on something that wasn't there. Her hair was missing in spots, although colored brown, revealing her age. Her dress was creased and soiled with an apron over it, showing smudges and grease marks from cooking.

"Come in," she croaked as I mounted the stairs.

I extended my hand to greet her, but she didn't return it. She just stared at me behind tortoise eyes that were buried a hundred years deep into her sockets.

"Come in," she said again, "do you think that I have all day?"

My feet felt as if they were weightless, drifting me across her doormat. I attempted to hold the door for her, but she nudged me from behind while saying "Go on, go on". I looked around for my brother as she slowly hobbled behind me. I turned to greet her.

"Hi, I'm Steve," I said.

"So you are," she muttered in a low, parched voice.

"It's a pleasure to meet you," I said.

"Same," she said.

"So I take it you're Mrs. DeFarge?"

"I am," she said.

"And do you serve meals here?" I asked her.

"I do," she said. "I'm cooking right now! Why don't you please have a seat in my parlor?"

Somehow, I knew which direction to go as I entered her parlor. It was a large room with chandeliers and oriels masqueraded behind red velvet curtains. I could feel the age-old history of this sitting room from its heyday.

"Where's the bathroom?" I asked.

There was no answer, as she was gone. I saw a hallway leading into a dark chamber. I proceeded that way. I checked a couple of doors out, hoping they would lead to a bathroom, when one opened quickly, and my brother appeared on the other side.

"Whew, Dan, I said. "I was worried about you."

"What's the matter with you?" he asked.

"Dan, this is pretty freaked out, man! What the heck are we doing here?" I asked.

"I thought you wanted to eat, Steven? We can eat here," he said.

"Hey," I said, "I'm afraid of what she might serve us."

"Why?" she asked from behind me.

I jumped, as I found this old lady standing right in the darkness of the hallway.

"Go have a seat," she told me. "It will be worth your while."

It was nearing six o'clock when she appeared again to lead us off to a back dining area. I couldn't help to wonder why I didn't smell anything cooking all of this time. She sat us in a long room facing her backyard. She had candles lit in seven places. There was a fire blazing in the stone fireplace set into the wall.

"What's for dinner?" I asked her.

"You'll see," she grumbled. "It's something that your brother won't have any problem eating."

As she hobbled her way back to the kitchen, I asked Dan if he had told her about his current bout with the GERD.

"No," he replied.

"How did she know that, Dan?" I asked.

"I don't know, Einstein. I called it in before we got here. Why don't you ask her yourself? What does it matter, Steve? I like this place. I like her. I feel safe here," he said.

"Hey, if you think we're all right, then I'm hanging in there with you, Dan."

Dan lit up a Camel. He found a floor ashtray off to the side and he moved it next to him.

"Do you think that it's all right to smoke in here?" I asked.

Dan did not respond. He didn't bother to look at me. Instead, he took a deep inhale of his cigarette, held it in, and then he blew it out in one long breath.

"Steven, come help me," I heard from the kitchen.

Oh, boy, I said to myself, as I stood up from my seat and went into the kitchen.

"Take this," she said.

She gave me two oven mitts to hold around a large black copper cooking pot. Whatever was in there was bubbling in a greenish, brown mixture. A sweet smell of turmeric and ginger was wafting out. I was about to ask her what this was, when she said, "Go!"

I carried it out and placed it onto a metal trivet

at the center of the table. I could see her backyard through the large picture window. Twilight was fading while trees outside were growing sinewy arms in the darkness. I noticed that her backyard bore a strange resemblance to Lilly White's backyard, but could not be too sure in the waning light. The fireplace roared its delight at our impromptu meeting from within its stoned, walled enclosure. Mrs. Defarge reentered the room with three bowls in her ancient hands.

"Could you go get the cups and bread, Steven?" she asked.

I returned with the items and sat myself back down at the table. She sat between the two of us. She passed a bottle of white wine. To my surprise, Dan poured himself a glassful. Dan was not supposed to drink while taking his medications, which was all the time. I told that to Madame Defarge, but she interrupted me in mid- sentence.

"Steven, I'm quite aware of your brother's condition. You are looking out for him like a good brother. Please," she said, "I would not harm either one of you. Believe me, it's ok. This wine will be good for him."

She stood up and was barely able to stretch out and reach the contents of the pot with her ladle as she asked me to hold each bowl. She dipped into what appeared to be a thick soup, which was one of the few things that Dan could digest at a time like this. We were finally seated and about to eat, when she spoke.

"It's my pleasure that you could make it here tonight. I don't get many guests anymore, since they opened up the new highway thirty years ago. Steven, you can eat, it's safe. It's lamb and vegetables blended together. I hope that you like it."

I looked to see Dan tearing into his bowl of lamb

stew with heaping slurps. There was soup splattering all over as usual. Much of it was landing on his beard. Mrs. Defarge never lifted her head.

"What's the matter with you, Steven? Are you scared to eat my food or are you wondering how much it will cost?" she asked.

How clairvoyant, I thought to myself.

"Yes, I am," she said. "So which is it?"

"It's both," I said, ashamed.

"Well, grow up. Can you pour me some more wine?" she asked me.

I ate reluctantly at first but found the soup to have a distinct taste of its own. Now that I had given in to her willpower and the possibility of being poisoned, I felt the over-powering need to find out why this chance encounter was happening.

"Madame Defarge, what is your first name?" I asked.

"It is Anne. Anne Marie," she answered. I said nothing.

"So, what did you think of that presentation last night?" she asked, catching me by surprise.

I looked at Dan, thinking what Tony had said to us, about speaking to strangers down here about the entity.

Dan answered, instead. "It was great. It was what the world needed to see."

Anne turned her small head with multiple chins and wrinkles waving, and looked at me.

"What about you?" she asked me.

"I was there. It was the greatest," I said.

"I know," said Anne. "So you believe?"

"Yes," Dan said. "We both believe, and we both talk to him."

"That is good," she said. "I am an old lady. I have waited for something like this for a long time. I have seen much in my lifetime. This coming of the entity is a miracle for the world."

"Can I ask you, Madame Defarge, about your name?" I asked.

She looked at me for a few seconds and then replied that she was wondering when I would get to that question.

"My mother was an avid reader," she responded. "There wasn't much to do out here a long time ago between travelers and carriages. She was reading *A Tale of Two Cities* at the time of my birth. She loved Dickens. That is how I got my name. I do not knit like the story character, although I do convey messages to others."

I was taken back by that last remark. *What did she mean by that?* I thought. I looked over at my brother to see his response, but he was still eating.

"Can I ask you one more question, Madame DeFarge?"

"Go ahead," she said.

"I have a very strange feeling about finding your place here tonight. It seems that it was meant to be, like it was preplanned. How did you know I was at the observatory last night and what my brother could eat?" I asked.

"You must remember that life can be mundane, day in and day out. It is often taken for granted except for your birth and then again, your death. This shall serve as a reminder to you that anything is possible, anything…Steven. I would be lying if I told you that I didn't know certain things. Just keep an open mind, Steven. There are things that people know that may astound you. Do me a favor now, Steven, would you help me get the tea and the Entenmanns from the kitchen, dear?"

After our tea, Dan went to the bathroom again. Madame Defarge then leaned her small head towards me and said in her gurgled voice that she had something important to tell me. The glow from the fireplace sparked her image onto the wall, resembling a wild chicken pecking about.

"You were wondering, Steven, about some of the things that I knew about you and Daniel?"

"Yes," I responded, seemingly in a trance.

"Well, my Steven, there's a lot to wonder about in this thing called life. You will see things that appear as dreams. Do not misinterpret them or take them for granted. Your dreams may be more real than you are. There are many things that we do not see and are not aware of. That does not mean that they do not exist. Your dreams can be your pathway to enlightenment. Things will happen that you must believe in."

She then leaned over even closer to me, her lips and breath brushing my skin. Her shadow flickered in spasms, from the firelight onto the walls. I could smell the years of garlic, sweat, love and musk, as her words nibbled upon my ear.

"I must leave you with a secret, my dear, Steven. You may have trouble accepting this, but it is true and you will have to find a way to live with it."

She motioned with her tiny finger for me to move my ear even closer towards her mouth. I did. Then she whispered her secret in my ear. My heart pounded in my chest.

SIXTY-TWO

We were back at the campsite at nine-o'clock. I started a fire in our pit, and we sat around it for an hour. We couldn't stop talking about Anne Marie Defarge. It was more than slightly unreal how we came across her. Was it strictly coincidental or fate? Did the entity have anything to do with it? Dan was engrossed with her and could not stop talking about her. They did hit it off for some reason, as if they had known each other or were expecting to see each other. This whole trip was growing tentacles around us, as if the coming of the entity was not earth shattering news by itself. It seemed that our daily lives were now also becoming part of an elaborate fantasy that had somehow woven itself around our alien visitor. While Dan kept on about her, I couldn't stop thinking about the secret. I wondered if she had also told my brother. I was tempted to ask Dan, but doubted what good it would do.

Dan retired early to the van at ten-o'clock. He was exhausted. He was in the van smoking his cigarettes with the lamp on. I could hear his radio playing softly in the background. Oogie and I sat near the campfire, while I watched the stars above through the smoky haze in the trees. Oogie was lying down as I went to the tent to retrieve my sweatshirt. There was a damp chill in the air.

As I returned to the fire, I found Oogie standing and growling at something.

"What, boy?" I said. "What do you see?"

I was straining my eyes to find what he was barking at. My first thoughts turned to an animal of some kind, perhaps a bear, possum, or raccoon. I grabbed

Oogie by his collar and attached his leash to it. The last thing that I wanted was for him to go running off to attack some other animal. Oogie's hair was now rising on his back while his growling increased to a feverish pitch. I couldn't see or hear anything beyond the crickets and wind. I thought of going back to the van and locking the doors, but that sounded too sensible of a thing for me to do.

So I listened instead but heard nothing. He was now keying in on something, as his body shifted slightly and began to shake. His tail was standing straight up. My senses told me to run, but my feet were not cooperating. I moved Oogie out to the dirt road surrounding our campsite to get a better look. It was too dark, though, to see anything.

I tried to go back to the tent to get my flashlight, but I couldn't budge Oogie. He was pulling me back to the roadway when I thought that I saw something. I stopped in my tracks. I could feel my heart pounding as Oogie tried to pull me closer. I thought that I saw it move again. I was certain of it this time. There it went again. It was a light or a glimmer of something bright that was flickering between the trees. It seemed to be coming closer now toward us. *This can't be a flying saucer*, I thought. *Not now. Not here. Not after all that has happened.* Whatever it was, it was actually approaching me by way of the road, only giving the appearance of moving from tree to tree. Something or someone was walking down the road and coming my way.

I still thought about the flashlight in the tent. Then I saw the well pump in the ground off to my side. I quickly pulled Oogie over to it and slid the handgrip of his leash over its handle. I was able to secure him for the time being. I ran back to the tent and retrieved my flashlight that was lying on the floor. I ran back to Oogie, took his leash off the pump and put it back into my hand. I lost track of the light that was coming our way. Whatever it was must have stopped and turned off its light. Perhaps they saw us? They must have heard the barking, though, long before?

I decided to turn on my flashlight, even though we would be giving away our exact position. Of course, it didn't work. It never worked when I needed it to work. I was about to open it and check the batteries when I realized that I had Oogie in one hand, and he was pulling me forcefully. I had to grab the leash with both hands in order to restrain him. It was at times like this that I wished I had a gun for protection. *Oh, well, too late now!*

Whoever this was must be able to hear that I had a dog with me. That should have deterred them. But no sooner did I think that that the light went on again, and began advancing towards us. *It was a lantern*, I thought. I could see it swaying back and forth. I could make out the faint figure of a person, a shadow behind the glow. I was ready to call out to the figure but couldn't find the courage.

Everything around me seemed pitch black, except for my campfire, which was throwing wicked shadows. I could hear footsteps nearing me as they crunched on the pebbles and stones on the dirt road. Then it stopped again for some reason. This was driving me crazy. This person stood silently as Oogie became frenzied and was backing up. Whoever it was began to walk forward again toward us. We were only twenty or thirty feet apart.

"Hey," I screamed, "you better stay right there."

That seemed to get its attention as it halted again.

"What do you want?" I screamed. "Who are you?"

I heard a voice saying something.

"What did you say?"

"I was taking a walk," repeated the stranger.

"Well, you'd better stay back, because my dog is going crazy."

"Can I speak to you please?" it asked.

"Well, let me see," I said, as I inched closer. "Hold on."

I was probably a good twenty feet away. I could make out the figure much clearer now. It was that of a short person, no taller than five foot, four inches.

"Why don't you stay still and allow me to approach you with my dog?" I said.

The voice called back, "Okay."

Oogie was uncertain about moving any closer. He went a foot and then backed up again. Slowly we made progress. He sniffed the air around him wildly, becoming less apprehensive with each step. We stood about three feet apart and Oogie became hesitant to go any closer. I was able to see that this person was wearing a hooded sweatshirt of some sort that was covering its head, creating a ghostly, monk-like apparition. A voice from behind the lantern said, "Hi!"

"Hello," I said back. "What are you doing walking around this park in the dark? You either have to have a lot of guts or be crazy,"

"Well, I'm camping here tonight and I must have gone the wrong way after leaving the bathroom. I saw the campfire and thought that it was mine. I'm really sorry for the commotion I created. I heard the dog barking and I got scared. I froze and shut off my lantern, not knowing if the dog was loose or wild."

"You have a lot more courage than me to be walking out here by yourself in the middle of the night!" I said.

I could now gauge from the voice and the outline of the face that this person was a woman.

"I know that it's crazy, but I do crazy things now and then," this person said. "My name is Jess."

"My name is Steve and this here is Oogie. Hi, Jess. I think he is calm enough to meet you now, if you move real slow," I said.

"Okay," she said, as she approached us slowly. She stuck out her hand for Oogie to sniff. Before too long, he was wagging his tail and allowing her to scratch his head.

"There, that's better," she said to Oogie. "Good boy."

As she stood a few feet away from me, accented in the glow of the campfire, I could see that she was wearing a baseball cap underneath her hooded sweatshirt. Immediately, I thought about that lady who supposedly was following me around. I must have jumped back in my surprise.

"What's the matter?" she said. "It looks like you saw a ghost!"

"Oh, no, I was just thinking of something that startled me," I said. "It's nothing. I'm okay. So how long are you camping here, for?"

"I'm only here for tonight. I've been doing the Antique Trail thing this week."

"You're kidding," I said. "We've been doing that, too. Listen, I really have to tie Oogie back down to his post by the fire. He's pulling me in order to get to you again. Why don't you come and sit with us by the fire?"

"Okay," she said. "Are you sure that you don't mind?"

"Not at all," I said. "Come and join us."

I could see her more clearly now as we walked towards the glow of the fire. Orange flames cast a Halloween silhouette upon her face. She was definitely an attractive lady, perhaps in her forties but with a more youthful appearance. She had a dark complexion and bore resemblance to a native American Indian She wore dungarees, hiking boots, and a rain poncho that covered her hooded sweatshirt, concealing most of her face. Under the poncho, her hood created the apparition of an Arabian lady wearing a turban with its many layers and folds, helping to shroud her identity from this world. But her eyes could not be concealed. They were vivid and piercing. They were cobalt blue and shining, reflecting the dancing lights of the campfire.

Meanwhile, I kept on thinking that this was the lady that my brother was talking about. I thought about going over to the van and asking Dan to come out and have a look but realized that my brother would probably tell her if she was, and I wasn't certain if I wanted her to know that yet. I wanted to keep this a secret for now. What if she wasn't the lady? That could be embarrassing. But what if she was? Would I be better off withholding the fact that I thought it was her? This was getting like a cat and mouse game, or a poker game where I had a hidden ace in my hand and she didn't know. I decided right then and there not to ask her at this time.

"So how long are you camping here for?" she asked.

"Oh, I'm only here for one night, too. Is it Jess?" I asked her.

She nodded her head up and down as she said, "Yes."

"I was just going to make myself a cup of hot chocolate, Jess. Would you like some?" I asked her.

"That sounds great, Steve, if you don't mind."

"Not at all. You know, I'd really like to talk to you," I said.

"Are you camping here by yourself, Steve?" she asked me.

"No," I said. "I'm with my brother, Dan. He's probably asleep in the van right now. We've had quite a trip so far."

"Oh, really, how do you mean?" she asked.

"Well," I said, "why don't you pull up that chair, and I'll tell you. It would be a lot warmer around the campfire."

I went back to the van and got a saucepan, some water, and packets of hot chocolate. I could see that Dan was sound asleep with his radio on. I couldn't help but think about this chance encounter of meeting Jess here. Or was it by chance? Who would be walking alone in a deserted state park at this time of night? It didn't sound plausible. Then again, what if she was the lady who was following me around? What if she just wanted to meet me? What was so wrong with that? Maybe she was just shy, like me? What could this lady possibly do to harm me? Then again, she may be a complete stranger and not that lady.

I brought the items back to the campfire and pulled my chair up next to the fire pit. I set up a makeshift stand to mount the saucer upon and began to boil the water.

"So, where were we?" I asked.

"You were going to tell me about your trip so far, Steve."

"Oh, yeah, that's right, Jessica. My brother and I went on this trip to get away from our nuclear power plant up where we live, because we were afraid that it may get sabotaged. I suggested that we should take a long- awaited diner trip that we had been planning for years, while at the same time hitting the Antique Trail. But some of the things that have happened along the way have been amazing, unbelievable, and totally unexpected. So you came down here for Antique Trail Days, too?" I asked her.

"Yes, I did. I heard so much about it that I wanted to do it, too. But I don't think that my trip has been as eventful as yours."

I stood up to pour the boiling water into two cups of hot chocolate. I handed one to her and was about to sit down when she asked if I had a spoon to mix the chocolate with. I went back to the van to find a spoon. *Only a woman would want a spoon to mix her hot chocolate*, I thought, as I returned to the fire. She was sitting back down in her chair also, seeming to have stood up to throw something into the fire. I handed her the spoon.

"So, Jessica, where are you from?" I asked.

"I'm originally from the city of angels, Los Angeles. My dad worked for the service, and we traveled around the country with him. I guess that I was one of those army brats. And I don't mean to correct you in a negative way, Steve, but my full name is not Jessica, as you have been alluding to. It is Jess. Don't worry about it, because a lot of folks do that. Everyone assumes that Jessica is my full name, but it's not. It's kind of strange, but my real name is 'Jesusa', or translated to English, is Jesus. It's Spanish, you know? You've heard of men called Jesus in Spanish. It's a very popular male name, and my mom is Latina, and she wanted to call me that."

"Oh, I'm sorry, Jess. I didn't know that. I won't do that again. That's the first time that I heard of a female named Jesusa."

"That's all right, Steve. Like I said before, don't worry about it. My mom was hoping for a boy, so when I came along she decided to just add an 'a' to the name, and that was that. My mom and dad were very religious, and our family has always added a Jesus to each generation. I happened to be the last link in this generation for that to happen, so here I am!"

"Wow," I said, "that's very interesting."

Jess finished stirring both cups of chocolate and handed my cup back to me. "Cheers," she said, as we both raised our cups up.

"So where do you live now?" I asked her.

"Well, I'm kind of in between places right now. Currently, I'm staying with some friends in Pennsylvania. I guess you can call me a nomad."

"And you've come down here, all by yourself?" I asked.

"Yes, I have. Why, do you think that that's dangerous, Steve?"

"Well, these days, Jess, yes I do! There's a lot of crazy things going on in this crazy world of ours," I said.

"I take care of myself, Steve. I seem to have a good sense of when trouble is around. And you, Steven, are you single?"

"Yes, I am. I was married once before, a long time ago. I guess you can say that it didn't work. And you, are you married, Jess?"

"No, Steve. I can't say that I ever had the pleasure."

"Hmm, that's strange," I said, "wouldn't you say, a pretty woman like yourself?"

"Well, it happens. I never felt right about anyone. I don't know. It must be me. So, Steve, what do you do for a living?"

"I'm retired from the government, Jess, social services. What do you do?"

"I work with the church, also doing social work, mentoring, along with inspirational therapy. My job involves a lot of traveling. Perhaps that's part of the reason that I have never settled down."

"Listen, Jess, I hate to interrupt, but it's getting a little chilly out here. Would you care for a blanket? I was going to get one out of the van for myself."

"Sounds good, Steve, thanks."

I came back with two blankets and handed her one. I also moved my chair closer to hers.

"Why, don't we get a little closer to the fire?" I suggested.

We both inched our way closer. I found it interesting that our jobs were so closely related. My mind drifted back to who this woman was. Could this possibly be the lady that was following me around? If she was, she was playing me also. I didn't mind. The more that I spoke with her, the more I liked her. There was something about her. I didn't know what it was, but I found myself drawn to her. And I didn't mind that, either.

I was taken from my thoughts as Jess took her baseball cap off to reveal a mound of curled black hair in a braid. She placed her hat on her lap as she shook it free. She pulled it back into a makeshift ponytail and then pushed it through the opening of her cap backward on her head. I found myself spellbound, staring blatantly as her hands seemed to move in slow motion. She noticed my interest and smiled back at me.

"That feels better," she said.

"Tell me something, Jess? What do you think about this entity thing?" I asked.

"Well, I definitely think that it is real," she said.

"Have you spoken to it, Jess?" I asked.

"Yes, I have, and how about you, Steve?"

"Yes, my brother and I have both spoken to it. It seems that most of the people I have met and know have spoken with it. Only down here in these parts have I come across people that haven't. But the strangest thing of all, is that my real life is becoming more unreal since the entity has come."

"What do you mean by that, Steve?"

"Well, like I said before, we've been having some amazing things happen to us on this trip, things that seem unreal. You may think that I'm crazy, but I'm going to say it anyhow. Lately, I've been having trouble separating fantasy from reality. I mean, when I dream, I think that I'm up, and some of the things that have been happening seem dreamlike."

"I'm going to surprise you by saying this, Steve, but I know exactly what you are talking about. The same has been happening to me. I haven't had the adventures that you've had, but my dreams have also been more real. I don't know exactly what it is, but I have my suspicions. I think that the entity is trying to show us the connection to our dream state and what lies beyond."

"Yes, I agree," I said. "Do you also talk to him about life and death, Jess?"

"Sure, don't you think that most people do, Steve? I mean, don't you think that it's only normal for people to ask an alien, our first visitor from another world, all of those questions about what this really is? We want to know what it knows. What are the secrets?"

"Yes, I agree, but there are some people who don't care or don't want to know," I said.

"Yes, Steve, those are the ones that he leaves alone. He knows that they don't want to be approached. They are probably the ones who are closed-minded. They believe only what they were told to believe and cannot accept anything else. Don't you think that God would want you to learn things, know more, and expand your knowledge? Don't you think that he would want you to use that precious thing that he gave us, our minds, our brains? Why else would he have given it to us for?"

"You seem to make a lot of sense, Jess. I do agree with you."

I was thinking about the old lady and desperately wanted to tell Jess about her, about the secret. But I couldn't.

"What's the matter, Steven? You seem worried," Jess said.

"Oh, it's nothing, Jess. I was just thinking about this old lady that we met this evening. We were looking for a place to eat dinner and..."

"Don't tell me that you found Madame DeFarge, Steve?"

"Yes, we did," I said.

My ears began to ring. I was getting that strange sensation again, of surrealism. I sat there next to this strange lady who had walked out of nowhere in this park tonight, who was now adjusting herself under this blanket that I had given to her. Who was this person? I felt as if I was dreaming again or was drugged. I was staring at her as she smiled serenely back at me. *How is it possible, what are the chances that she, too, could have found Madame DeFarge and her reclusive hideaway? What else does this strange lady know that I didn't know?* I could hear her voice and it sounded heavenly, suddenly far off.

I could see the ebbing fire as it jumped in her cobalt blue eyes. I could feel the weight of my eyelids turning into five-pound dumbbells, crashing down on me, while my legs turned rubbery and numb. I felt as if I was going to pass out. My body seemed to be levitating from my chair. I could swear that Jess had put her arm around my shoulder, but I was drifting off into slumber. Her lips were moving, but I could not hear.

SIXTY-THREE

Lying in the tent half way between dreaming and daybreak, a cool breeze blew upon my face as I let my mind wander through recent fresh dreams and foggy reality. I could smell dawn, the heat of the sun burning upon the new canvas tent roof, and the freshness of the surrounding pines. There was the scent of smoldering embers in the fire pit, with a hint of Turkish tobacco from my brother's cigarette smoke from outside. I could feel Oogie next to me as his wet tongue sloshed across my face with the machine-like precision of a pair of wiper blades in a fierce rainstorm. With that realization, I awoke immediately.

"Holy cats!" I exclaimed, as I crawled out from under my blanket. Somehow, I couldn't remember how I wound up in the tent with my sweats on. I had the weirdest sensation that I was dreaming of some girl named Jess last night. Was that true? I found myself asking Oogie, who looked at me as if to say, "I can't talk, Steve. We've been through this before, haven't we?"

"Do you want to go out Oogie?" I asked. Now I was talking his language. He bolted up, wagging his tail. I opened the screen door zipper of the tent and let him out. Dan was sitting outside in the folding chair, enjoying that much needed first smoke of the day.

"Hey, Dan," I said. "Did you see anyone around here?"

"Yeah, Steve, the boogeyman just left, and he told me to leave you a message."

"All right, Dan, I take that as a no. Thanks, Dan," I said.

I had to go to the bathroom and quickly found

my shoes neatly stored with my clothes by the front opening of the tent. I looked at them quizzically, not remembering leaving them there. I rushed to put them on. I had to go badly!

"Let's go get breakfast," Dan said upon my return.

"All right," I said, "but I don't want to go back to Madame DeFarge's. I'd be scared of the omelette she would whip up."

Dan laughed as he took in a deep inhale. I was taking the blanket out of the tent when a hair binder fell to the floor. I reached down to pick it up. I was certain that I met some one last night, but it didn't seem real. Was I going crazy? I could smell a faint hint of perfume as I folded up my blanket. I must have fallen asleep in my chair last night. Maybe it was something I ate?

Oogie and I walked the campground that morning one final time. I went around looking at every site, trying to find some bit of evidence of another camper. There wasn't another soul in the park. I noticed that my cups were in the van where I usually kept them. They were next to the saucepan, with the packs of hot chocolate. Everything was in its place, except for two packets that were missing from the box. I was trying to remember if that was a new box before last night. *Oh*, I said to myself, *let me check the fire pit*! I gazed into the embers. I moved it around with a stick. There were no traces of it.

I stopped on my way out of the park at the ranger's office.

"Hi, we're leaving today," I said.

"What site were you in?" the ranger asked me.

"I was number 122."

"Okay. Thank you, Mister Shapiro. Have a nice day."

"I was wondering if my friend ever made it into the park last night," I said. "Her name was Jess."

"I don't think so, Mister Shapiro. You were the only camper here last night."

SIXTY-FOUR

In light we see, in light we are seen.
The flames dance and our lives are full.
But as night follows day,
the candle of our life burns down and gutters.
There is an end to the flames.
We see no more and are no more seen.
Yet we do not despair, for we are more than a
memory slowly fading into the darkness.
With our lives we give life.
Something of us can never die:
we move in the eternal cycle of
darkness and death, of light and life.

Kaddish at Rosh Hashanah

Dan was sitting at his kitchen table, smoking his first cigarette of the day. From the look on his face, it must have been a generic. He was playing with his pills, lining them up and counting. His hand reached for his water between puffs, but he put it down again. He went from short, quick drags on his generic to raising and lowering that glass.

"Come on, Dan, I'm hungry. How about the diner?" I asked.

"I'll be ready in an hour," he replied, preoccupied. "Come on, Dan, I can't wait an hour. I've been waiting for you to get up all morning long."

"I can't go," he said between puffs.

"Why not?" I asked.

"I have to wait for my meds. The drug store may deliver them at anytime," he said.

"Dan, they don't come until after three. We've got plenty of time," I said.

"All right, give me an hour," he replied.

"Dan, I'm leaving with or without you in a half hour."

We were back at our diner in our usual seats being greeted by the host and the manager, Ali.

"Where were you guys? I missed this guy," Ali said, as he squeezed Dan's shoulder playfully.

"We were in West Virginia," Dan said. "Let go of me now!"

"We were hoping you were all right," said Ali. "I forgot that you left. You missed the attack on the power plant. We had traffic out here for two days."

I returned Ali's big smile. It made me feel good to know that he cared about my brother. He led us to our customary table in the back and stood aside, as we sat and waited for our waitress.

"I love this guy," Ali exclaimed, as he couldn't help but try to grab Dan again from behind.

"Get off of me," Dan said as he feigned total annoyance and wrestled with his hands to free himself from Ali.

"I can't believe this guy," Dan said.

Ali was now running his hands through my brother's hair, irking him even more.

"Come on, Ali," I was forced to say. "Give the guy a break!"

Ali was now re-combing Dan's hair back in place with his hands in retribution.

"I can't help it, Steve," Ali said. "I just love this guy so much."

"What are you guys having?" asked Lynn, our waitress, who came up to our table.

"I'll have a BLT on rye toast and a diet cola," I said.

"Well, Dan, what are you going to have, and don't give me that soft and gooey bit," Lynn said.

"I'll have a tuna with cream cheese on white, with a Sanka," Dan said.

"You got it, Dan," said Lynn, as she retreated into the kitchen to place the order.

"Hey, Dan," I said. "That was easy! How come you ordered that normal style today?"

Dan studied me for a while before he answered.

"I guess because it wasn't eggs, Hitler! Any more questions, dictator?" he asked huffily.

"All right," I said," I'm sorry, Dan. I didn't mean anything by it. That's one of your favorites, the tuna and cream cheese on white."

"And did you know, Steve, you used to talk to yourself in the mirror when we were growing up?"

"Yes, you've told me so, Dan, many times. How come you never told me that when we were younger?" I asked.

"Well, I never wanted to embarrass you, Steve. You were a little dictator back then, too. I'd hide in the closet laughing hysterically as you made these threatening, long speeches. You were going to beat everyone up on the block. It was too funny to ruin. I didn't want to stop you. I'd wait till you left the room, and then I'd come out of the closet. You still make speeches, don't you?" Dan asked.

"Well, Dan, yes, I do, but mostly in the car, now. On that note, let me ask you something about Grandma on Dad's side," I said. "When she was dying in the hospital, did she get you alone and tell you that she thought you were going to be famous?"

"No, why, did she tell you that, Steve?" asked Dan.

"Yeah, Dan. She made Mom and Dad leave the room and she told me that at her bedside. I thought she was telling every one of her grandkids that, just to make each one feel special. It was a pretty good ploy on her part, if she did that. But I never forgot it. It left a lasting impression on me."

"Are you kidding me, Steve? You didn't even speak until you were four years old. They took you to a doctor to see if you were retarded or something! Didn't you know that?" asked my brother.

"Yeah, Dan, only because you've told me that many times before. Just as many times as you've told me that your IQ was over one hundred and sixty. And just as many times as you told me why I was never told my IQ score."

"And why's that, Steve?" Dan asked.

"Because it was under one hundred, and nobody wanted to hurt my feelings, you've said."

"Oh, yeah, I have told you that, you're right, Einstein," Dan said, as he giggled.

"But, Dan, I'm not kidding. I remember looking in her eyes when she told me that. She was serious, I think. What made her think that?"

"Maybe she was delirious by then, or perhaps she thought that you were some other grandchild, Steve. I don't know! They say that morphine can do pretty weird things to you, you know, Steve? So what did she actually tell you? Do you remember?"

"Yeah, Dan. She said there was a feeling that she had. She could just sense it. And me being the stupid one! I still think she was just trying to build up my ego, knowing that I was the weak duckling," I said.

"Well, you never know, Steve. Maybe she knew something or felt something. You never know? You're not as dumb as you used to be!"

"It's funny, though, Dan, that, here we are now, and I'm taking care of you. Who would have ever thought that, huh?"

"Yeah, Steve, you've come a long way for an idiot dictator."

It was great to be back at our diner.

SIXTY-FIVE
The Last Dream

"Consider this to be the number one question most asked of me. What happens to you when you die? This is what humans have asked me more than anything else. Before I go, I will tell you as much as I know," said the entity.

"Okay, so why do we have to have the TV on to do this?" asked Dan. "I don't like watching TV."

"You don't have to, Dan," advised the entity. "You can see everything in your mind just as well. I thought it might be more convenient for those who want to see it on TV, Dan, much like a movie," replied the entity. "If you don't want to watch it, you don't have to. Your world has become a boob-tube civilization, what can I tell you? Your brother Steve looks like he doesn't care. Is that right, Steve?"

"I don't care," I said. "I would rather watch it on TV, I guess."

"Well, then, this is it, guys. I may never see you again, at least not in this life of yours! I stand corrected. I may never speak to you again! So call this my final tribute to you and all of mankind. This is my going away present, my final curtain call."

"So this is it for us? You're out of here after tonight?" I asked.

"Yes. I have places to go and things to see, kind of redundant of me, you know," said the entity.

"Well, I guess I don't get around much anymore, like you," I said. "I'll just hang out here for awhile longer. If we never speak again, it's been quite a revelation. I'm only glad that I lived to see such a thing."

"Same here," said Dan, as he lit up a Camel.

I was allowing Dan to smoke in our den for the night, so that he wouldn't have to get up to leave the room for breaks. But in reality, I knew that once it started, he couldn't smoke, even if he wanted to.

"It really doesn't matter, though," said the entity, "as Dan will be mesmerized once we get going. Let's just hope that he doesn't put a burn in your chair."

"Would you kind of keep an eye on him for me?" I asked the entity.

"Always," said the entity. "I'll make certain of it, Steve."

"Stop your worrying, Steve, all right! I'm not gonna put a burn in your chair," said Dan.

"Well, when is it starting?" I asked.

"It already started for half of the population. I can wait. Whenever you're ready," exclaimed the entity.

"Okay, I'm ready," I said.

I had the television set on at a very low volume. The TV station was blank and fuzzy, similar to when the station has gone off of the air.

"Here we go," I said as Dan nodded in agreement.

And just like that, I was dreaming, boom! I was looking out of my apartment at 985 Anderson Avenue in the Bronx, and it was 1955. I was a little guy, so I had to stretch to see out of that window. There was my brother Daniel, running up the street toward our building being chased by Frank Bailey. Frank was a bigger kid, maybe a year or two older than my brother. Dan was barely holding his own and was now heading up to the front steps of our apartment building. When I mean bigger, I mean fat. Frank was shaking and baking. What I mean was that he was coming like a steamroller out of hell. For a fat guy, he was all a-jiggle. His breasts jolted up and down with each footstep, running. His waistline and pants turned wildly from side to side. The fat on the back of his arms were jostling, like jello wobbling.

I left the window and ran to our front door of the apartment on the second floor, so that I could let Dan inside, ahead of fat Frank. To my surprise, my fifteen-year-old sister Carole had already heard the commotion outside and was waiting at the top of the second floor landing for fat Frank.

My brother was running up the steps, fear on his face, as fast as he could. Not far behind him, turning the corner to go up the steps was fat Frank, all two hundred plus pounds of him. Dan ran past my sister and into the apartment. I watched as big Frank was hitting those steps in stride, head down and chugging for a fat boy. Now, by no means was my sister frail and weak. She was zaftig, in Jewish terms, meaning that she was a big-boned girl. I watched in utter amazement as Frank hit the final step on his way up, picking up his elephant-sized head just in time to witness a vicious two-arm thrust into his neck.

The fat guy went backwards down all sixteen steps, rolling like a sinister looking Mister Slinky toy, while somehow managing to get up to run away. I knew then and there not to give my sister any crap! I was in awe of her, as well as in fear of her! When she said to do something, she meant to do it. I tested this fact out one other time, and so my prized toy garbage truck went down the incinerator, never to be seen again in this lifetime.

Temporarily, I snapped out of my dream while still sitting in my recliner in the den. I turned to look at Dan, but he was no longer sitting in the chair next to mine. *Am I still dreaming this right now?* I thought.

"Yes, you are, Steven," the entity replied. "I am still with you,"

"Where is Dan?" I asked.

"He is also in his own place now. Don't worry. I want you to learn more about your dreams and the afterlife. I want you to see the connection between both."

"You were again with your brother and your sister in another time, a time that is just as much alive as this present time. I want to send you back again, Steven, to other loved ones who have never left you. You are still with them throughout eternity. The memories have never died."

I started to dream once more.

Out of nowhere, my deceased grandfather Kalman was standing over my shoulder playing his fabled clarinet. I was spellbound and didn't have words to greet him with. He was telling me to stand up in his heavy Yiddish accent and to play my saxophone with him. Out of nowhere, my saxophone was sitting next to me. I stood up and slid my neck strap over my head. I started to wet my mouthpiece when I heard my grandfather break into a rendition of "My Yiddisha Momma." I looked up from where I was standing to see that I was in a rather large ballroom, filled with relatives and old friends. It was a wedding from the '40s.

My mind was swirling as I picked up the rhythm and joined in. My dad was sitting directly in front of me at a table with my mother. They appeared to be in their thirties. I saw a baby sitting on my mother's lap that must have been Danny, and next to him was a little chubby girl of the age of six, my sister Carole. My dad was tapping his feet to the rhythm while nodding his head. I looked to my right where my grandfather, short and stout, with a bulldog face, and cheeks puffed out from blowing the clarinet, gazed in my direction, signaling for me to take the lead. I began to play a solo to the song. My mom and dad were now dancing directly in front of me on the crowded dance floor, as he turned her to the beat of the rhythm.

Somehow, I managed to hit the right notes as I watched them glide across the floor. My fingers moved on their own, up and down the sax, as my grandfather put out his hand to signal me to stop, while wearing a wry smile upon his face. This joy of just playing with my grandfather was overwhelming.

"What is this?" I called out to the entity.

"You are dreaming, Steven. You are with the loved ones in your life, again."

"Where am I?" I asked. "This feels much too real."

"You are where your dreams go, Steven. Yet you are still seated in your recliner in the den."

"How is this possible?" I asked.

"This is all possible because life does not end. The essence to life is with your loved ones, along with the love that you show on this earth. Death is not the end but is a living thing that is passed on forever through new generations of newborns. Those memories that you make, you leave behind and take with you. I don't know exactly where your souls go, but I do know that they never end. Your dreams, your mind, and your soul are the connection to eternity."

"This all has something to do with my secret, doesn't it?" I asked the entity.

"Yes, it does, Steven."

"Am I still dreaming?" I asked.

"Yes, you are," said the entity.

"Where is my brother?" I asked.

There was no answer.

I stood up, feeling suddenly weak and groggy, like an old boxer in the tenth round of a twelve-round fight. Upon rubbery legs I searched through my area of the house looking for Dan but could not find him. I then went looking in his apartment. His lights were on as usual, but he wasn't around. He wasn't outside on the porch where he usually smoked when the weather was nice.

"Where is he?" I asked again.

"He is neither here nor there," the entity replied. "He is in his own dream now, Steven."

"I don't know what that means!" I screamed.

The television drew my attention as I saw my deceased mother and sister speaking to me. It showed me sitting on my bed while they both stood at my sides. They appeared as I last saw them. My sister was a mere twenty-five years old, tall in stature, attractive with dark hair. She bore a striking resemblance to Lilly, except for the color of the hair. My mom was sixty-seven years old, a broken woman from the loss of her only daughter, my sister. They appeared now, as if they had never left. I was reaching out and touching them. They sat next to me and both draped their arms around my shoulders.

Always together, I said in my thoughts. *You two have never been apart.*

They both smiled at me.

"Where is he?" I asked them. "Where's Dan?"

They did not respond.

Their images began to vibrate, much like a movie projectors, skipping from a worn-out film. Then, they began to fade from view until they disappeared from the screen. They were gone, just like that. I was alone again. I stood up and continued my search for Dan. I found myself in his bedroom. His room was a mess as usual, but I had the feeling that he was watching me. I looked around in desperation. I thought that I heard a muffled laugh coming from the closet. I figured that the joke was finally over. I opened the door, but he was not there.

I noticed his opened wallet lying on the floor. Through a plastic sleeve I could see a note that had been written in Dan's handwriting. I opened it up to read it. It said, "We'll be around." I spun towards his dresser and could smell his clothes inside, as if he was standing behind me. There were photos of our family laid strewn on top. One recent photo of Dan in this apartment showed him content and finally at peace again. He held his bearded chin in his palm, and his eyes brimmed with love. This was my brother as I used to know him. These were the same eyes as when he was younger and happier.

I found my way back to my recliner. I was weak from emotion. I looked over at where my brother was previously sitting. The cushion of the seat still had his impression wedged in it. The cigarette that he was smoking was now smoldering in the ashtray, a mere butt.

SIXTY-SIX
THE FAREWELL PARTY

It was a Friday evening in the summer of whenever, but does it really matter? It was a week after the entity gave its rousing farewell to mankind in regard to our search for God and the afterlife. It was the end of a long, hot, peculiar summer. Man had seen more natural disasters and changes then ever before. The Earth was blessed with our first alien contact. But it wasn't as people expected it would ever be. It was more of a backdoor surprise. Oh, well, it only goes to show you that you never know what you're in store for. Never assume, an old friend had once told me.

There were still many doubters. After all the substantial proof that was provided, there were still those that could not believe. Doesn't that sound vaguely familiar? What else is new? Whatever, many were celebrating mankind's greatest moment. Unofficially, this Friday was anointed as Earth's first anniversary of rebirth. If others still couldn't believe, then life would go on as it always has.

For us though, it was a celebration. It was a celebration of life. Nobody on Earth had heard from or made contact with the entity since last Friday. I was in the den with many of our friends. There was Bryan and his newfound girlfriend Gina. It seemed that Bryan had found a new perspective on life. There was Charlie and his girlfriend Maureen, so similar to the Charlie that we had met in West Virginia. The only person missing was my brother, Dan.

I had told everyone at the party how Lilly and Dan decided to get together for good and relocated to her house in West Virginia. For I had thought that may have been what happened after my brother's sudden disappearance on the night of the entity's farewell.

I went into my brother's apartment again during the party and smelled his musty clothes, the stale cigarette air, and the hints of coffee brewing. I looked at that photo of him, which I'd be keeping forever. That look of love in his eyes would be my lifelong memory. The mass of poetry books, of which I would keep a few, a reminder of his quest for fame as a poet, as a person, to be a something in life. I felt as if he was looking over my shoulder, yet somehow still communicating with me. I could feel him hiding behind the closet door, while holding back from laughing out loud. I shook my head to clear my thoughts.

What is reality? I thought. I found myself waiting for the entity's reply.

Oh, well, I said, *it's back to the party*. This was, in fact, a farewell party for my brother as well as for the entity. Little did my friends know of my surprise when I called down south to speak to Lilly about Dan's vanishing. Her phone was disconnected a long time ago.

"No such number," was the reply. I was so confused and despondent that I called the local sheriff's department in Canton and spoke with an old-timer on the police force. I asked him if he would be kind enough to go check in with Lilly, at Eberneezer's? He laughed! He told me that that would be pretty hard to do since the place closed down back in the `60s. I asked if he would call her up, out at her house in the country. At this point, he asked me if I was some kind of a practical joker. I said no, just old family trying to get back in touch. He said that the house was razed many years ago after Lilly disappeared with some guy.

"She's never been heard from again," he said. I found it hard to stay focused on what he was saying. Now the old lady's secret was starting to make sense. In a flustered state of mind, I asked one more question.

"What's that?" he said.

"By any chance, would you remember what that guy's name might have been, who she ran away with?"

"Well, I think I do. Give me a second, now. I use to be good friends with old Eberneezer. Now don't hold me to it, but I think that this fella's name was Don, yeah, Don. No, wait a minute. It was Dan, I think! It's been such a long time."

I remember after hanging up the phone that I stubbed my toe really hard against an old brass kettle lying on the floor. I hit it so hard that I knocked its heavy weighted lid off. After rattling to a rest, I noticed that someone had placed a neatly folded fortune from a fortune cookie inside of the kettle. *Who would have done that?* I wondered, as I bent down to unfold it and read it. It said, "Look for the dream that keeps coming back. It is your destiny." Though unimaginable, I knew who left it. Peculiar, though, since my brother could never fold anything that neatly! It had the touch of a woman.

Returning to the party, I sat back in my recliner, holding onto my brother's wallet that he apparently left behind for me to find. I dreamily looked at its contents once again until I came upon the other note that Dan had left me. That was the one that said "We'll be around." I thought of the secret that old Madame Defarge had told me. She said, "Your brother will be leaving you for a very long time, a very long time. He will be going back to a better place, another time, where he will be healthy again and happier.

It will only take an instant my dear," she said, as her ancient lips brushed against my ear and she whispered, "just in the wink of an eye." I was thinking of that secret when I heard my friend "Little Mike" say to me that someone was at the front door waiting to see me. I stood up slowly, gallantly holding back my tears as I walked across the living room floor, stumbling as I went..

Who can this be? I thought, as I approached the partially opened door. Through the crack I could see the rain from the glare of the streetlamp above. It cast a sinewy shadow over the feint silhouette of a slight woman in a hooded sweatshirt, with thick curly hair and cobalt blue eyes, under a baseball cap.

The End.

Author's Note

This story was completed in memory of my real-life older brother and story character, Daniel Shapiro, who passed on during the writing. Dan was five and a half years older than I, and did in fact become a challenged person at the age of twenty-seven after living a normal life up until then. I admired my brother throughout his life, which was a tough one. He was one year short of graduating from Brooklyn Law School in New York when he decided to hitchhike to California in the late `sixties and he lived there for three years. Daniel changed physically, mentally, and emotionally upon his return home. He lived his new life in New Jersey close to me, alone in rooming houses, hotels and efficiencies. I looked out for him as best as I could, but he always allowed me my freedom. My brother gave me inspiration by showing me how he struggled to get up everyday and tried to be a success like anyone else. He tried to find his way through the pen and the notepad. Dan wrote poetry for thirty-seven years.

He wrote everyday and always had a notebook with him.

Daniel died of a massive heart attack on January 20th, 2008, at the age of sixty-three. I was present at the time. Dan died when I was writing the part where he meets Lilly White. He had finally met the girl of his dreams, as he so often wished. Dan and I lived together for the last two years and four months of his life. We were both happier. We would go to our favorite eatery, the Riverside Diner, whenever we could. This was Dan's favorite pastime. He would actually drink five to six cups of decaffeinated coffee and smoke many "ciggies" while there. The owner's son, Ali, would often sneak up behind Dan and hug him. He was loved at that diner. I would often comment to Dan that this was like being two kids again living in the house alone, with no parents around and doing whatever they pleased. We had the best two years and four months as brothers.

I did in fact, actually find that exact fortune cookie fortune, after knocking the lid off of an old brass kettle, the week of his death. I will miss you, Dan, for the rest of my life. You will be in my dreams and heart and will hopefully be hiding in all of my closets while listening to my speeches.

"We'll be around."

ADDENDUM

The idea of *Entity, A Second Coming* came to me in a dream one night while camping in Montana, in 1999. I dreamed about my brother hearing the entity's voice for the very first time. I wrote the dream down the next morning. I did not begin the writing of the story until my brother moved in with me in 2005. Each subsequent chapter was written from dreams or when I gained fresh insight after awakening in the morning. My brother did pass away during the writing when he met Lilly, who I characterized from our older deceased sister, Carole. His untimely death changed the format of the remainder of the story. After completing the first draft, I went back to include his death as a significant part of the ending. That, too, came to me in the form of a dream. It was almost as if he was telling me to do so. I find it compelling that my brother sought success through his writings, due to his limitations and challenges. On the other hand, I never had an urge to write until I dreamed of my brother. In a very strange way, I believe that my brother played a huge part in the writing of this story. He was a very intelligent person and I wouldn't put it past him, if he somehow found a way to use me as a conveyer for this purpose. In that light, dreams do come true.